GOD

OF

RAIN

*"Lives do not wrap themselves up
as neatly as the epics of the storytellers."*

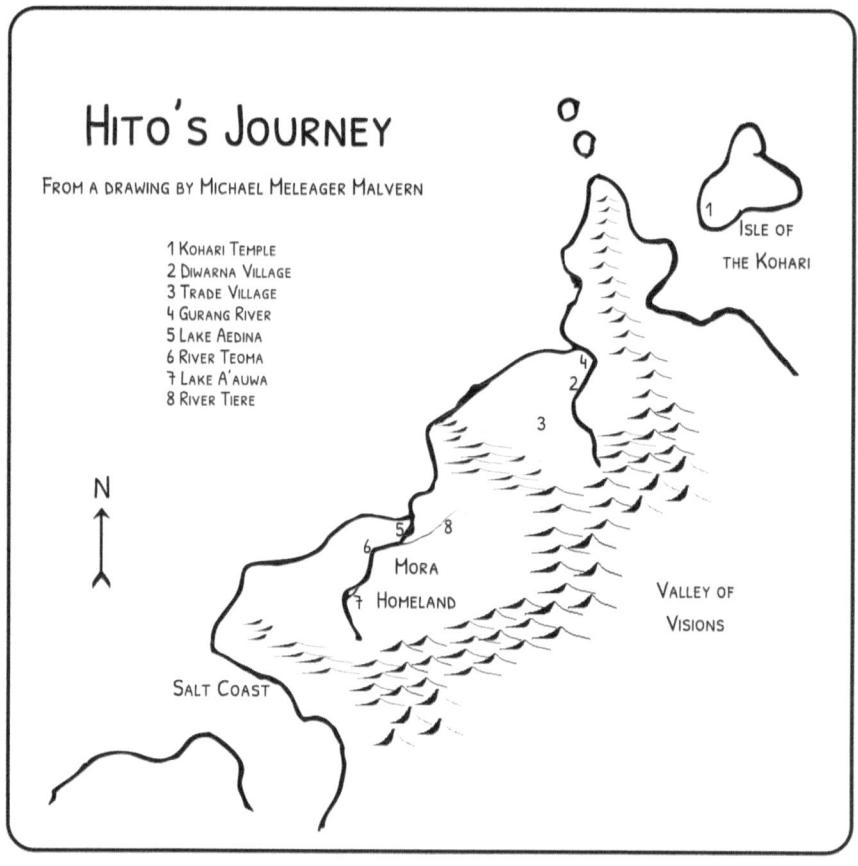

HITO'S JOURNEY

FROM A DRAWING BY MICHAEL MELEAGER MALVERN

1 Kohari Temple
2 Diwarna Village
3 Trade Village
4 Gurang River
5 Lake Aedina
6 River Teoma
7 Lake A'auwa
8 River Tiere

N

Isle of
the Kohari

Mora
Homeland

Valley of
Visions

Salt Coast

God of Rain
Stephen Brooke

Arachis Press 2017

God of Rain
©2017 Stephen Brooke

ISBN 978-1-937745-40-0

Arachis Press
4803 Peanut Road
Graceville, FL 32440
http://arachispress.com

Part I. The Search

1. Rebels

Would Aranu never learn caution? Once again, he charged headlong at the rebels arrayed against us and we had no choice but to follow.

Without me as his second, to order our troop for battle, the son of King Hei'iro might long since have been laid beside his ancestors. I say this as a truth. It is my duty to serve Lord Aranu as best I can.

Our foes broke and ran. This we expected, for they were but rabble, commoners who no longer had a leader since the death of the mad King Hara'a nearly a year before. Few rebels remained, guided — or misguided — by a handful of fanatical priests, while a new king stood on Hara'a's dais.

Commoners. I say this almost with contempt, do I not? Yet I, Hito, am a commoner as well, never to rise higher than the second for some noble commander. Not unless I might elevate myself into the nobility somehow. There are ways to accomplish this but I shall not speak of them now.

A shrill blast of the bone whistle that hung from my neck called our men back to us. This was a tactic I learned of the Taona

Marareta, the Hero from the Sea, so I can not claim it as my own. But it is true that I was first to use it in battle. It is easier to hear than the conch horns the Mora have long used for signaling.

"Any injuries?" asked Aranu of the assembled warriors.

"I think I stubbed my toe tripping over a body!" came one cheerful response. No, nothing serious, a cut here and there, bruises. The inevitable broken fingers; those were always vulnerable in a hand-to-hand struggle.

Only three prisoners were brought before our commander. Any enemy too badly injured to stand would have been dispatched. Mercifully would they be, as befits any man brave enough to engage in battle. "These two knelt in surrender," I reported to Lord Aranu. "The other was grabbed as he attempted to run." This latter scowled at me.

"Take oath to no longer oppose the High King and you may return to your homes," Aranu told the two submissive peasants before him. "Poneiva grants this to any who will swear truly."

The men swore readily, eagerly even. Perhaps they were as tired of war as I, but had seen no way to break with their fellows. It was good that High King Poneiva was willing to pardon such rebels. We would feed them — they looked nearly emaciated — and send them on their way, home maybe to loving wives and families. Or maybe not, but at least to freedom.

Lord Aranu turned to the third prisoner, considering him for a moment, looking the lean little man up and down. "A priest," he said. That was evident from his tattoos. "Were you anything other, I would sentence you to slavery. But not a priest." He pondered a moment more and then nodded to the man who stood behind the captive. A swing of a war club and it was over.

"Is there wood enough for a pyre?" asked the young nobleman, not bothering to look again at the body.

"No, my lord," I told him. We were in the midst of a grassy savanna. "We must dig a grave."

Aranu dug with the rest of us. That was his way.

As we rested that evening, sharing a cold meal, I asked, "Will we pursue that band?"

"No, Friend Hito. They can be King Naire's problem now." We were well into the lands of Naire, the kingdom once ruled by Hara'a. The man who had been chosen to rule now was a somewhat distant cousin, an older man who had never expected to be named a king. He seemed a good leader, an honorable one. But one never knows.

"I shall send a messenger," Aranu continued. "The rest of us can return to Poneiva."

"And then home?"

"It is to be hoped." He looked up into the starless heavens. "I fear it will rain all the way."

It was that time of year, and expected. "If it starts up again," I said, "the men would just as soon march as try to sleep in the rain."

He nodded. "Let us get what rest we can while it holds off." With that, he rolled over and seemed to fall asleep immediately. I could not.

What would home hold for me? My Lord Aranu's wife and little daughter waited in the house of King Arierona, but I had only my duties among his warriors. Even my friend Rika and his master, the Taona Marareta, would no longer reside there. I should visit Marareta before journeying home.

Yes, Aranu would not mind that. I would mention it when we returned to the High King.

2. A Parrot

A string of obscenities greeted us at the house of the High King. "Palala is here," remarked Aranu.

"Then it is likely the Lord Beka is visiting his brother," I replied. The men had already been given leave to find food and beds in the great, half-finished structure. They knew where.

The green and yellow parrot regarded us balefully from its perch on the veranda, before again cursing in both Mora and Kohari. I liked the easy-going yet valiant Beka but did not care so much for his Palala. The bird had been bought from a Kohari trader, on the beaches below the Great Falls.

Beka himself greeted us at the entry. "Poneiva is busy being talked at by his new High Priest. He should have picked one who knows when to shut up. Come along." We followed him down the broad hall, between thick, square-hewn posts reaching up to the highest ceiling I had seen in a building on this side of the mountains. "I wanted a High Priestess," Beka whispered to us. "Everyone said it had never been done but couldn't give me any reason why." He shrugged. "I think my brother missed an opportunity!"

"Poneiva is more of a traditionalist than his predecessors," spoke Aranu.

Beka nodded. "I don't know much of such things. And try not to learn. Oh," he added, "your father sent a message that he wants to see his new granddaughter soon."

"So do I," Aranu said. It had been a season since he had led us from the house of Arierona to serve the High King.

"I think Poneiva will be sending you home. Ah, here he comes." The High King strolled toward us, surrounded by priests, their high feathered crowns bobbing as they made their farewells. Poneiva's own red and gold crown rose above them all, as did he. The High King was a large man, though not so huge as his late cousins who had held the dais before him.

Beka might have been born in another land — another world, Marareta said, though I do not understand that — but he was as tall as and even broader of shoulder than his adopted brother. Not so inclined to fat, however; I suspect the Lord Beka will remain lean as long as he breathes.

And Aranu was not that much smaller. It looked like the start of a wrestling match when he embraced the High King, and I would not have given odds on which would be victorious.

"Come and eat with me," said Poneiva. "You too, Hito." There are many nobles who would not have included me at their meals, even ones who profess to have left the old traditions behind. But I had known Poneiva since he was no more than a boy. He was still young, to be sure, only a little older than Aranu, but had always had a certain weight and dignity to him. And ambition; anyone could have known he would be more than another minor noble-man's son though none would have predicted him on the High King's dais!

I took my place, as befitted my rank, to the right of my three companions, and added little to their conversation. The roast pork and yams took most of my attention.

"So we shall send you back to Arierona and your family," Poneiva was saying. "It is not good to miss seeing your child grow."

"And maybe you can start in on adding another one," said Beka. "Amirea misses you. I arrived from Arierona's house just two days ago." He did not add that both his wife and that of Poneiva yet resided by Lake A'auwa, awaiting the completion of the High King's abode. There was no need.

"My Lord Aranu," I spoke, "perhaps I could part with you for a while and visit the Taona Marareta." It seemed as good a time as any to ask.

Before my captain could reply, Poneiva jumped in. "I am told the taona is visiting my cousin Temani'itu. You should journey to the Great Falls if you wish to see him."

"I am heading there myself," added Beka. "Travel with me." Had Aranu any intention of objecting, which I doubt, it was too late.

"I would gladly journey with you again, Lord Beka," I replied.

"Excellent," said the High King's brother. "We leave at dawn."

Poneiva stated, "You must take along a couple men, both as protection and as reminder of your station. You should not have traveled all the way from A'auwa alone."

"I wasn't alone," laughed Beka. "Palala accompanied me. But he had best remain here until I return."

Poneiva sighed.

3. The Taona

Marareta would always remain a stranger in our land. Perhaps that is why he had friends among the Kohari and would visit with them beneath the Great Falls.

It had been a quick and easy trip by canoe, down the Teiri to the Teoma, and then on to Lake Aedina and the house of King Va'aru that stood on its shores. The flooded rivers flowed swiftly.

Now we stood below the cliffs that flanked the Falls, on the wide sand beaches where many great canoes rested, and greeted the Taona Marareta. Unexpectedly, not only my friend Rika stood with him but also Samua, the cook turned priest, who had once served as Marareta's attendant. Why would he leave his island in Lake A'auwa?

"Temani'itu is out to sea," the taona told us. "He and Neatanu are trying out his new canoe."

"It is the biggest canoe ever built!" claimed Rika.

Marareta chuckled at his aide's enthusiasm. "In this world, perhaps. Come along to the house of all who sail upon the sea." This long, low building served as home to many of the Mora who served Temani'itu. It was open on all sides but here and there hung mats dividing it into rooms of a sort. Men sat in groups or slept in hammocks beneath its thatched roof.

I knew that this house was rebuilt from time to time, for the great storms that came from the sea would carry all away that lay beneath the cliffs. The canoes would be filled with rocks and some would survive and others disappear into the waves.

A nobleman I did not know came forth to give greeting, tall but lean and burnt dark by the sun. He squinted at us from below a craggy brow. "Ho, Naio, I have come to make you uncomfortable again," called Beka.

So this was the Lady Pua's surviving husband, Temani'itu's second. Beka's greeting was intended in jest, I am sure, for Poneiva sometimes spoke of giving his brother command of the fleet when Temani'itu's leadership ended. Naio understood this and understood as well that Beka had no such ambitions. He grinned at his supposed rival.

"Lord Beka, you are welcome. More so as you have left Palala elsewhere!" He turned his eyes to me and the two warriors who had accompanied us on our journey here. "Welcome to all." Above the cliffs, many a nobleman would have not deigned to even notice us; here, among those who sailed, things were different.

Rika laid a hand on my arm. "Let us walk," he said, "and tell each other our stories." Much had passed since last we spoke.

We left the others at the long house and walked along the beach, gossiping of many things, his family, my battles, the doings of our friends and enemies. "You will return now to the house of Arierona?" he asked.

Would I? "I do not know, Friend Rika. I am weary of war and weary of serving. It may be time for Aranu to find a new second."

"And you to find a wife, maybe?" Rika joked but he knew I had been thinking of marriage ever since we both returned from across the mountains.

"Maybe. Those are Kohari traders across the lagoon, aren't they?" I shielded my eyes from the sun and peered over the water at the huts and the unmistakable shapes of the traders' boats, so unlike our sleek Mora canoes. To my eyes, they looked more like baskets.

"They are." He considered the swiftly flowing water, the discharge of the rain-swollen Teoma into the sea. "Best we not try to swim across. There is a way beneath the falls."

Either way, we were thoroughly soaked by the time we reached the other side. No matter; the sun was high and hot. "That is Poyo," spoke Rika, gesturing toward one of the open huts. "He remains here almost all the time and acts as agent for those who bring goods. Poyo is a friend of the taona."

"Ho, Rika," called the paunchy Kohari merchant. "Come to ogle my daughter-in-law again?" A smile showed itself within his gray beard.

"Not when your son is watching," came Rika's lighthearted reply. "This is Hito, my friend. Marareta's friend, as well. They have been companions in journey and in war."

"Then he is welcome. More so if he has aught to trade."

I admit that I knew little of the trade that occurred here below the Great Falls. Of the overland commerce with the Diwarna, I was familiar, the exchange of woven mats and crocodile hides and a hundred other items. But what did the Kohari bring by sea?

For that matter, what did they take back?

There seemed to be much jewelry and other ornaments displayed, amid more utilitarian trade goods. As we looked them over, with no great interest, Rika suddenly stopped and whispered, "Do you recognize those stones?" He nodded toward a small selection of translucent, colorless rocks. My face surely betrayed my bafflement. "We saw them in the Valley of Visions."

Oh, yes. The two of us had visited the mines there. We were the only ones in our party interested in such things — Rika simply because he was naturally curious about all things, I because I recognize the value of knowledge. "It is one of the stones they mix to make their weapons," I replied, also keeping my voice low.

"The Lord Bafa will be interested in these. He seeks a source of such stones."

"We should trade for some." I looked toward Poyo. "What do the Kohari want?"

"They appreciate anything well-crafted. Baskets, carved wood. That's the sort of thing that is easy to carry home profitably. But I have nothing with me."

Our interest, try as we might to hide it, did not escape the Kohari trader. "Some consider those jewels sacred to the goddess Lugan, the Morning Star. Perhaps your wife would like one, Rika."

"In truth, Friend Poyo," replied my companion, "I think my master might be interested in seeing one. The Lord Marareta is interested in novelties of this sort." I had not known Rika had it in him to bargain so, using the name of the taona.

Nor had Poyo, it seemed. He laughed before speaking. "For the Hero from the Sea, I will give the stones as a gift. In truth, Friends, no one wants them very much. Most desire quartz or obsidian. However," he continued, "we would not mind a pig or two finding its way over here. We grow tired of dining on fish!" The merchant picked up two of the stones and handed them to Rika.

"For Marareta, we thank you. He sometimes plays for us on the sef he obtained from you."

Poyo's smile at that was broad and genuine. "I would gladly make music with him again sometime."

"Sir," I asked, for I might as well, "do you know the origin of these stones?"

The Kohari considered this request, obviously not comfortable with the idea of revealing the source of his wares but knowing it truly mattered little. "They were gathered on the the coasts south of here, beyond the hills that divide Mora lands from the sea."

I nodded. "I know those rocky shores. There is little there but the nests of seabirds."

"My people rarely visit them. It is far from our home."

And they would be aware the Mora would slay any they caught on those desert coasts.

4. Canoes

Temani'itu's new canoe was, in fact, two great dugouts, carved from the massive jungle trees of the Gurang, placed side by side, combined as one vessel. Lord Neatanu had told him of such craft in his own world and Temani'itu had to have one, for he had long desired to build the largest canoe ever known. Now, the brother of the late High King Maitoa could take pride in the knowledge he had done so. Temani'itu was not young, and so bulky that he walked with difficulty. He might not command the fleet of the Mora much longer nor, for that matter, remain in the world of men. It was good that he could look upon this great canoe first.

We feasted with him that night. I suspect the Kohari feasted as well, for Taona Marareta made sure to send a pair of pigs their way. He showed small interest in the stones we had found, saying only that they should be delivered to Bafa when we returned south. I think maybe Marareta did not like things to change too much, did not like the idea of bronze weapons becoming common on this side of the mountains.

But who can change what will be? They would come to us, sooner or later, and it would be best if the Mora knew the secrets of their making. I was the only one of the warriors who had visited the Valley of Visions to bring back a sword of bronze, the others deeming them too heavy to carry over the peaks. It has served me well, but perhaps I should cast it and all the things of war aside now. That was to be seen.

Samua sat unobtrusively a short distance behind Marareta, rather than taking a place with the other guests. Here, he would have been welcome to join in as an equal. Lord Naio looked long at the little man before saying, "You are unlike the others who came from the sea, yet you seem neither Mora nor Kohari. Are there those like us in your land?"

"There are, sir," spoke up Samua. "Not relatives of mine, though. I think." He seemed uncertain about this.

The man who had once led those who came to us from the sea, Neatanu, said, "There were rumors among the men that your mother was Chinese. I think that was just guessing." I do not know what Chinese is but it must be a tribe of their homeland. When Samua continued, he used many words I did not understand. Marareta explained them to me later, but they still seem strange.

"But a good guess, sir. I did learn that my mother was an whore from Chinatown. Died of consumption, she did, when I was just a baby, and I was sent to the orphanage." Samua slowly shook his head. "I don't remember her."

Neatanu considered this. "Then you are not very closely related to any of the people here. These Kohari are obviously descended from one Malay-speaking group of people or another."

"More than one, maybe," spoke Marareta. "Who knows how many small groups might have passed from one world to another over the centuries?" He amended that to, "Over the millennia."

Turning to Naio, the taona went on. "I have little doubt that your ancestors came here from my world." He smiled thinly. "Or as the great sorcerer across the mountains would have it, one much like it."

"Fleeing an enemy, the legends say," spoke Temani'itu. "Exiles in nine great canoes."

Marareta had once told me he believed the story of 'nine canoes' was made up later to match the nine kingdoms of the Mora. This is something I can believe.

He told me also of his belief that we of common birth had more Kohari blood in us than anyone was willing to admit. That bothers me not one bit. Whoever my ancestors might have been, they had their lives and I have mine.

"We must take to canoes in a day or two," said Beka. "Up the Teoma to our homes. Or to my brother first in my case, and then home as soon as I can."

"I'll be going with you," Neatanu said. "Back to my wife and to Andarua at the house of Va'aru."

"You have not stayed long, Beka," grumbled Temani'itu. He was fond of the young man and probably favored him as his successor, though he would not say so in front of Naio.

"I had to come see your great canoe," explained Beka. "I expect to sail in it when next I visit."

"That you shall. You leave too, Marareta?"

"Yes, back to my house." There was something in the way he said this that betrayed — weariness? sorrow? Not so long ago it was the home of his great friend Hareata, slain the year before by rebels. Now Marareta dwelt there and had taken Hareata's sister, widow of the High King Maitoa, as his wife, as a matter of duty. "Your wife is there, Naio. Come and visit."

Naio sighed. "I should. I neglect the Lady Pua." That Pua and Marareta had been sometime lovers was of no concern to either man. That seemed long ago, now. Very long ago.

5. *Rumors*

Before taking to the river, one must ascend the cliffs and walk the paths to Lake Aedina, above the Great Falls and the lesser falls further up the Teoma. All of us save Samua could clamber up the stout ropes — the plant from which they are braided was one good thing we obtained from the Kohari. The old cook was hoisted in a basket.

"We could hardly tell he was there," claimed one of those who pulled him up. "If only Temani'itu were so easy to lift!"

The high roof of King Va'aru's house rose before us by the afternoon. Aedina lay calm, misted by light rain. On the broad porch overlooking the lake sat Va'aru himself, smoking a great bamboo pipe, occasionally exchanging words with attendants who came and went.

So like to his slain cousin, Hareata, was he. I started to mumble a prayer for the dead man but could not think for a moment what god to address. Why not the Sky, that rules over all?

"Welcome," he called to us, not bothering to rise. "Eat with me tonight." He turned his gaze back to Aedina. I think maybe there was much kalina leaf mixed with his tobacco; that is the same plant from which we make our ropes.

I found myself with Samua on one of the side porches, both seeking food. There is always a buffet at the house of any great lord, day and night, to feed both guests and retainers. We filled bowls with fruit and taro paste and cold fowl, and found mats overlooking the king's gardens before he spoke. "I do not sit down to feast with the rest of you because the beer would be too great a temptation. Drink would have ruined my life, in time, had I not come to this land of yours." He paused, perhaps thinking of things that might have been. "That is one reason I chose to join those priests on their island. But I don't really belong in the middle of Lake A'auwa."

"Have you found where you do belong, my friend?" I asked him.

"I am looking." He chuckled. "As are you."

Maybe everyone is, I thought, but this I did not say. "Your friend Andarua is here, is he not?" I asked instead, casually, between bites of papaya. It might have been riper.

"Friend? I suppose. We spent much time together when we first came to your land, for we could not travel with the younger men. But we have not much in common.

"Yes, he is here and remains the man of Neatanu, as he has been much of his life." He shrugged. "I do not know whose man I am. Perhaps I shall stay with Marareta again, for a while."

"We need wives to take care of us," I told him.

"Ah, yes. Women was the one thing we lacked on that island!"

Samua, despite being little, ugly, and bald, would have no problem finding a wife, should he wish one. Any number of widows would find him acceptable. But what of me? Had my ambitions made me too critical of my choices in the past? Those ambitions seemed less important now.

When I turned to speak to my companion again I found that he had fallen asleep. So worn he looked!

Samua did not appear at Va'aru's meal that evening but I was there, sitting well below my noble fellow-travelers. Andarua I could see, directly behind Neatanu as was normal for ones attendant. And there sat Neatanu's wife, Hueta, across from us with the other women. She looked little like her daughter Amirea, wife of Aranu, being angular and broad of shoulder.

I sat further down but not so far I could not hear the conversation of the king and his noble guests. And Rika attended Marareta; I could depend on him for more details later. There were rumors, I heard, rumors of unrest among the Kohari.

"They are becoming bold again," claimed Va'aru, "after their great defeat three years ago, and see our recent turmoil as weakness."

Marareta spoke plainly. "It was weakness. We were fortunate there were no attacks while we fought among ourselves."

We. He spoke of himself as Mora now, and why not? Even if he could never be completely one of us in his heart, even if finding a place and a bride had also brought him great loss and sorrow, Marareta deserved to be considered as good a man of the Mora as any.

"There should be closer watches on the coasts," said Beka. "I spoke with Temani'itu of these things." I might have known he had reasons to visit other than seeing a new canoe.

There were sounds of approval all around and more drinking of beer. They served good beer in the house of Va'aru, good Mora millet brew. Yet, at times, I had a yearning for the beer I had drank for a season and more in that valley beyond the mountains, made of a grain Marareta named 'barley.' It was unlikely I would taste it again.

6. Wives

At dawn, we were paddling against the strong flow of the Teoma, leaving Aedina and headed south. It was not far to the house of Marareta but our progress was slow. We might have done as well to walk.

This was rich country, the heart of the Mora realm, here in the kingdom of Va'aru and those that lay above it along the river. There had been little fighting here. The people were contented with their lives.

Many small villages rose along the banks of the Teoma, amid groves of fruit trees, and many small streams flowed into the greater one. But there was little wild forest left. Where I had been born and grew up, along the northern borders of Arierona's kingdom, one could still find the tall ancient trees that stood before ever a Mora dwelt in this land.

Another village appeared to our right, looking to me like all the others we had passed. "Farewell," called Beka from the canoe he and his two warriors paddled. They continued up the stream as we pulled in to the shore.

"No one to meet us," remarked Rika. We pulled the canoe well up onto the bank, beside several other dugouts. Perhaps he had expected his Hepetea to wait beside the Teoma for him.

I looked about. So this was the land over which the taona now ruled, was it? It was a far step up from being a humble priest, a man without wealth or station. Yet it surprised me not at all. Was he not the foreseen Hero from the Sea? Oh, yes, some might argue that Bafa or even Beka could claim that title. Or all three of them at once. But Marareta stood above the others. He always had.

We followed a dirt path beside a stream narrow enough I could have leaped across it, shaded by citron trees. A fish pond could be spied to our right. Ahead rose a not particularly impressive house on a low hill. I knew it was very old, built before the time of the first High King, and was once surrounded by a palisade. It still had the look of a fortress about it.

Marareta held this place as a vassal of Va'aru, as had Hareata before him. He had not sought this; his marriage to the late nobleman's sister, Panoha, had brought him here. For two seasons had Marareta mourned his slain Rahaita before taking another wife.

He had sworn to provide for her, but I know the taona also cared for Panoha. No, he did not love her as he had Rahaita but such love is rare.

A girl came out onto the porch, a baby in her arms. "Look Maratoa, your father is here!" she told the child, holding him up. Ah, the son of Marareta — and of Pana'a, the priestess who could never leave A'auwa nor take a male child to her sacred isle. He was a good looking boy, sturdy and black of hair.

The taona took his son from the girl. She was younger than I had first thought, no more than eleven or twelve years of age, but tall. "That is Tita, isn't it?" I whispered to Rika.

"It is. She loves having a little brother." Tita would be the daughter of Panoha and her first husband, the late High King Maitoa, which made her also niece of Temani'itu and of the Lady Pua. The latter now came from the house, with three other women, all clustered together as women tend to do. Panoha I could recognize and, of course, Rika's wife Hepetea. The other then must be Hareata's widow. What was her name?

And didn't they have a son?

By now, an obviously pregnant Hepetea was in Rika's arms. Even Samua seemed at home, chatting with Lady Pua about something. I was the one new to this house. "Come, Hito," called Marareta. "I must present you."

"This is the great Hito of whom I have heard so many tales?" asked the tall and slender woman beside him.

"Not from me," Marareta assured me. "The storytellers have spread your name and exploits." I knew that I appeared in Ulani's epic of our trip across the mountains. But I had only been a follower, then and since. Certainly no hero. "This is the Lady Mehetu," he continued.

"I greet the Lady Mehetu," I said, being carefully formal. I think she liked that.

"And you know the others, I believe," said the taona. "My wife, Panoha, of course." He sounded unsure, but I had indeed met Panoha before, though briefly. She was as I remembered, of good height and substantial build. Very much the sister of Lord Hareata.

My eyes returned to Mehetu. She was a bit ugly, wasn't she? But an honest ugly. Homely. That would be the better word.

"This is Tita," Marareta went on, pulling the girl forward. She gave me a frank and somewhat disconcerting looking-over.

Seemingly satisfied, she politely said, "Welcome to our house," and returned to little Maratoa, who was trying out his legs with some success.

"Toare is about somewhere," spoke Mehetu. "With the warriors I think." She turned to me. "That is the son of Hareata."

"A good boy," said Marareta. "A good young man." He seemed distracted, distant, but I knew not why.

7. Toare

"Stay with us here for a while," said Panoha, picking an oblong citrus fruit from the tray before her. "There is no need to hurry back to Arierona, is there?"

"I suppose not, my lady," I replied. I hesitated before saying, "I may leave the king's service."

"It's about time," muttered Marareta. He had not added much to our conversation this evening.

Here, he held the place of honor at meals, with Panoha to his left — a place Mehetu would have had a year ago. Now, the widow of Hareata must defer to both Panoha and Pua. That put her more nearly across from me.

Samua sat with us, a space above me in deference to his position as a holy man. Rika and Hepetea apparently did not take meals with the nobles, but I was a guest. "If you permit, I shall return to A'auwa with you," spoke Samua. His eyes went to our hosts. "This is not the place for me. Not right now, anyway."

"You are always welcome here, Samua," Panoha told him. "It is good to have someone like you about the place." She glanced at her husband and smiled. "Marareta completely neglects any priestly duties these days."

He only bowed his head to her in response. Conversation lagged. Marareta seemed uninterested and the Lady Panoha did not seem the sort to initiate anything. She was rather shy, I think, but she had much wit when she chose to speak.

That left things to Mehetu and me. "My lady, I have not yet seen this son you claim to have," I told her.

Her laugh was pleasant. I should try to awaken it more often. "He must play warrior and eat with the men. I would think he got enough of that in Anana's service."

"Anana?" This was the king who ruled the coasts north of Va'aru's realm.

"Toare is training under the guidance of King Anana's commanders. He will return to them soon." This was common for young noblemen. So did Aranu, the son of a king, end up in the service of another king, Arierona.

"He would rather be a poet," interjected Samua. "The boy should study with a master."

A sigh came from the noblewoman. "I would not mind. But Toare thinks this is expected of him." A frown, a slight hesitation. "It was what his father wished."

"And he has thoroughly thrown himself into it." This came from Lady Pua. "I think perhaps it is time I went elsewhere, too," she said, returning to our earlier topic. She might have been thinking on it as we had moved on.

"To the house of the High King?" asked Marareta. Pua nodded.

"But visit us," said Panoha. "Tita will miss her aunt."

The Lady Pua smiled broadly. "Young Tita could certainly visit me, you know. Poneiva would welcome her in his house. And you." Her eyes went to Marareta. "Tell your husband to take you along the next time he goes to see the High King."

Panoha also looked at the taona. "I think I shall not travel for a while. May I tell them why, Husband?"

"Certainly," he said. "I could scarce keep from letting the news out myself these past days." Marareta looked fondly at his wife. Perhaps he loved her more than I had realized.

"I am pregnant," she announced, and then laughed. "But the taona knew this was going to happen. There was a prophecy!"

"It is so," admitted Marareta. "Pana'a told me this." He grew suddenly pensive and lowered his head. "Excuse me," he said. "I must leave you." The taona rose and walked from the room, carefully placing his feet like a man striving to keep control of his legs.

We looked from one to another, wondering. "This day marks the anniversary of Rahaita's death," Samua whispered. "All this only brought up more memories."

"I know he broods on it sometimes," spoke his wife. "I do not mind that he loved her so."

We spoke little after that and soon I, weary traveler that I was, found my bed. But I thought I sensed someone standing at my doorway in the middle of the night, looking at me. It could have been a dream.

A young fellow of maybe sixteen years was eating breakfast on the porch when I wandered out the next morning. The house seemed mostly silent still. One look and I could tell he was the son of Lady Mehetu. He had the same oval face, the dark thick eyebrows, the slender frame. There was none of Hareata's bulk in the boy, though he was taller than I when he rose.

And then, his tattoos proclaimed his heritage as well. I myself bear few marks proclaiming anything.

"My Lord Toare, I assume," I said to him.

"You are the warrior Hito?" he asked. "The companion of Marareta?"

"Companion? I suppose. Is there any melon left?"

"I have heard of your adventures, across the high mountains and in the war against Hara'a. You fought in the great battle where he was thrown back!"

"I was there," I admitted. I didn't have the heart to tell the boy that the battle against the rebels was little more than a skirmish compared to those I had fought in on the other side of the mountains. No one here would have believed that many men would hurtle themselves against each other, not to mention the dragons and griffins that had taken part. I sat down and helped myself to dried fish and yams.

Marareta joined us shortly. He said nothing of the previous evening but began to pick through the fruit. The taona seemed to prefer the small sour oranges. "I thought maybe to accompany you south," he said, slowly peeling one of those he chose, "but it is not the best time." He raised his eyes to me. "You must give Pana'a my greeting."

"Certainly, Taona." Neither of us had anything more to say about that.

"Stay as long as you wish, my friend," he continued and then laughed. "But I know you will want to move along. Your spirit is restless."

"If only it knew what it sought," I answered.

"I sought a home, a place where I belonged in your land," said

Marareta. "In a roundabout way, I found one. I am almost content."

"Almost is not too bad."

I am sure young Toare was completely baffled by our exchange, but he had good manners. Marareta addressed him. "If Lady Pua decides to go to the High King I would ask you to accompany her, Toare. She should have an escort on her road and it is pretty much on your way back to Anana."

"I would be honored, Lord Marareta." The young man turned to me. "And I would be honored if you came and trained with me sometime."

Why not? "Let me know when."

8. Exercise

I would not exercise with young Toare today. I had been going too long without rest and might have no more opportunities to spend a day napping and drinking beer. Alas, those pastimes lost their charm by mid-afternoon so I walked in the garden, between rows of tall banana and papaya.

"Might I walk with you, sir?" came a soft voice.

"Certainly, my Lady Mehetu," I answered. She was very formal, was she not? That was not a bad thing.

We walked a while in silence. "I have no place here," she said finally. "I stay only through the kindness of Lord Marareta."

I knew that but had not thought on it. "He would never turn you out, my lady."

"No, he would not. He wants me here, I think. But not — not as a wife, you understand."

Was she thinking of marriage with the taona? I did not see that happening. Mehetu went on. "And that is fine. But it leaves me with no official status."

"Va'aru would always welcome you if things changed."

She nodded. "I know this, Hito. But I would be a ghost flitting through the house of Va'aru, with no station and no substance."

I could not help smiling. "It would seem your son is not the only one in your family who can turn a poetic phrase."

Mehetu laughed outright. "Was it too dramatic? I listen to the storytellers too much, I think." Then she added, in a more sober tone. "But it is true that I am no one now, and lonely."

"That is not right, my lady," I told her. "Not right at all." For a moment our eyes met and made promises.

Promises kept that night when Mehetu came to my bed chamber. She was gone when I awoke and I had no time then to think of all that had happened and all that it meant.

Marareta kept only a small troop of warriors here. Fewer than twice ten were practicing their skills in the exercise yard when I joined them and Toare that morning.

The boy greeted me by taking up a pose of challenge, brandishing his club and sticking his tongue far out, as did the warriors of old, in an attempt to look fierce. I would not tell Toare he only succeeded in looking ridiculous.

Men of the kingdom of Anana and other lands to the north sometimes strike such a pose, but more frequently in dance than in actual combat. I had seen them and had no doubt Toare had learned it there. We practiced for a while with spear and then with club; the youth was skilled enough but over-eager. That sort of thing gets one killed, unless one is Aranu. Toare would never be Aranu.

Pairs of men wrestled nearby. One large fellow watched us for a while before calling, "Come face a real man, Toare." There was scorn in his voice and in the look he gave me.

"Who is that?" I whispered to the boy.

"Taki. He sees you as a rival for my mother." Toare glanced at the man with undisguised distaste and went on. "But she does not like him. She should tell the taona to dismiss him from his service."

She would not, would she? Mehetu did not want to assert herself in a house where she and her son were now guests. Beggars, almost. I knew how that was; yes, I knew it well.

The boy continued, giving me a bit of a sideways look. "Mother likes you. You are serious." That he — and Taki — knew of the previous night, I had little doubt, but neither of us was likely to bring it up.

Perhaps I might discreetly mention the man to Marareta. Perhaps I could deal with him right now. "Toare does not confuse boasting with ability," I called back. It might have been foolish to do so. Taki was big.

And I am not, not by the standards of my people. It is true. The man did not reply but only motioned me toward him. The warriors formed a ring around us as I stepped forward. A silent ring — I suspected that Taki was not well liked by his companions. But I was unknown to them. The bulky warrior towered over me, hands opening and closing, ready to pull me into an inescapable embrace. I would not play that game with Taki.

I slipped to his left, took a thick wrist in both hands, put my foot against his ankle and took the man down. In a moment more, that wrist was behind his back and my arm wrapped around his throat. Ah, but it was not to be so easy.

Taki was fat but he was also powerful. He struggled back to his feet, with me clinging to his back like a child being given a ride. This would not do; the big man had all the advantage when we were both standing. Even more when he was the only one standing!

I slipped off and drove my knee into the back of his, taking him down again. This time I made sure to capture a leg, wrapping my own around it, and interlocked my fingers under a gargantuan jaw. Taki would not escape this, strain though he might. The powerful muscles of his neck fought surprisingly long against my grasp, his hands tried to reach back and claw at my face, but at last one wide palm slapped the dirt in surrender.

I have had opponents last far longer, men who knew how to wrestle. Yes, and some of those have defeated me but Taki had no skill, only size and strength. That can be deadly enough.

"Enough exercise for today," I told young Toare. "I need beer."

9. *Mehetu*

Mehetu stayed with me that night, and the next, too, my last in the house of Marareta. I knew that I and this reserved noblewoman were growing — what? Attached? I do not think we were in love, not really.

But she was the sort of woman for whom I had been searching. So I had claimed, once. Mehetu might be ten years older than I and probably could not give me children. Nor would settling down with her be likely to bring me the answers and the peace I sought. But, as the taona, I might be almost content.

She was the widow of an Ari Noe, a high noble, and therefor supposedly shared in his *mana* — some of which would pass to me if I married her, or even having slept with her now. I do not know if I believe in such things but there is no denying that marriage to Mehetu would elevate me to noble status and allow me to rise as high as my abilities could take me. Had not I always wished this?

"You leave this morning," she said to me, before the first light of dawn filtered through the grass-mat walls of my sleeping chamber. Nothing more did she say.

"I do," came my answer. "I must."

"Yes." There came a long pause. I heard only her breathing as she lay at my side. "You might return."

"It is likely." Marareta was my friend, as was Rika. I would sleep again in this house. But at this time I would not find the answers I sought here nor in Mehetu.

"Come back to me and we will speak of things," said Mehetu. I heard her rise. "I shall see you before you go."

There were two canoes departing that day, one bearing Samua and me, the other carrying Lady Pua and Toare. We would travel together for a short while. Before leaving, I spoke of Taki to Marareta, telling of his unwanted attentions to the widow of Harareta. I was not sure I should have, but I would be there no longer and unable to do anything myself.

The taona was wiser than I and might better know what to do.

Teoma was still in flood but not so high as a few days ago. The days of rain were lessening, though it drizzled even as we prepared to leave, as we made our farewells. My farewell to Mehetu was far more formal than I might have wished, but perhaps that was for the best. I would miss all of those who dwelt in the house of Marareta.

Then we were paddling south against the flow of the river. Would that the strong arms of Pua helped propel my canoe, rather than those of old Samua! In time, we reached the mouth of the Teiri, and she and Toare steered their dugout up its flow. I hoped that Lady Pua would find peace of her own in the house of the High King. She had lost much in the last two years, a husband, a brother, a son. There was little left to Pua.

War had taken it away, and I had helped make war. So things are. I was a warrior. I did not know if I remained one.

Days of paddling, then more days of walking, and Samua's chatter throughout. I paid him little attention. My thoughts were elsewhere. Some were with Mehetu. Some were across the mountains. Most visited our destination, the house of King Arierona on the shores of the great Lake A'auwa. As Pua, I did not know how my journey would end, what I would find there.

I only knew that I could never again be second to Aranu, the warrior I was. I must tell him so when I arrived and help him find a good man to serve in my place. Someone I could trust to keep that overgrown boy out of trouble.

Samua seemed weary as we climbed the path beside the high falls of Pana'a. What awaited him here was uncertain too, was it not? He had said he would not return to those holy men who dwelt on their rocky island above the falls. 'Munkas' he called them in his language, or something like that. Yet I knew he would always find welcome in the house of Arierona. Had he not served as guide for the daughter of King Arierona himself, Rahaita, on the night before her wedding to Marareta, keeping watch as she bathed in the Pool of the Moon below Pana'a?

Pana'a — I must speak to the woman who also bore that name, and give her the words of Marareta. I did not understand all that tied the two of them together. Now the waters of A'auwa lay before us, catching the grey-gold light of sunset through the misted rain. I could not make out the isle of the priestesses from here, where Pana'a led them in their dreams of prophecy.

Samua stood beside me, gazing southward. "It's good to be home," he said. But this was not my home.

10. Stones

I laid my two stones before Lord Bafa. They did not look like much to me. "Cassiterite," he stated. "Just what we need to find."

Marareta helped me with that word later. No Mora can pronounce it as did Bafa. "And they were found on the other side of the hills." He turned to more-or-less the proper direction. "Over there."

"Where we fought the invading Kohari," spoke Aranu. Both men had taken part in that battle, destroying a flanking enemy army that had landed in secret, but I had been elsewhere, with Arierona's main force. "I visited those coasts sometimes as a boy, further north where they adjoin my father's kingdom. Salt-makers had encampments there." Much of the salt traded among the Mora came from the realm of Hei'iro. The high cliffs and narrow beaches elsewhere were unsuited to its making.

"But they are deserted otherwise," spoke the king. "Inhabited only by seabirds. Did you ever see jewels like these there, Aranu?"

"No, my lord. But I was more interested in gathering the seabird eggs at the time."

"We should go over and look, I suppose," said Bafa.

Arierona nodded. "Do what is needed, my son." He paused a moment, then added a thought. "Take Hatiu. He knows the ways through the hills better than any."

"You must come, Hito," Lord Bafa told me. "You and I are the only ones here who would recognize these for what they are." He glanced up from the faceted stones to Aranu. "We will not take Aranu away from his family this soon after he arrived."

Aranu looked grateful. Bafa had learned the ways of leadership well, though he would never take the dais of the king who had adopted him. Some cousin would rule after Arierona, most likely the capable Ponu who had turned back Hara'a's invading army last year.

As for me, I had no objection to accompanying Lord Bafa. I had no objection to any direction I might go at that moment. "Choose some men, will you?" Bafa asked me. "Maybe ten or twelve will do. And provisions." The slender young man's pale face smiled at me. "In other words, my friend, I am putting you in charge."

I nodded my acquiescence. Bafa turned back to his stones, picking them up once again to peer at them. "They would make a good pair of earrings, wouldn't they?" he asked with a laugh.

Hatiu I found with no difficulty, lounging before a small hut near the king's house. He no longer served as a warrior but did know those hills and the ways through them as well as anyone. Or should I call them mountains? They were a spur of the high mountains I had once passed over, but certainly no more than hills at their north end. By either name, it was a rugged crossing.

By the time we set out, four days later, days during which I had no time for anything other than organizing our expedition, Bafa had thought to add a pair of bowmen to our group. I agreed that it was a wise precaution. He himself carried a bow slung over his shoulder, being the best shot of any man known. There were women, admittedly, who might challenge him, but none of those were coming with us.

"This will just be a scouting mission," Lord Bafa told me as we trod a gradually rising path toward the low mountains. Much of this was open grassland here, but we encountered more scrubby trees as we traveled south and west. "If we happen to find anything, that would be splendid, but I mostly want to learn the lay of the land over there. Your people name it the Salt Coast, do they not?"

"Aranu's people do, sir," I replied. "I've heard it called the Forsaken Coast here in the kingdom of your father."

"Hmm, that's a word I haven't heard much. I'll never speak the Mora tongue like those born here. But it's a good name for the place."

Hatiu guided us to a pass, the same one through which Lord Bafa and the others, including the traitor Nezama, had passed some three years before. It was the pursuit of Nezama that had later led us across the mountains, I and Marareta and the rest, so we might rescue Rahaita. I turned there in the heights of that pass and looked east. Might I return over those mountains someday, mountains that dwarfed those we now crossed?

There would be no reason, I knew. I could find what I needed here in my homeland. Down we went, toward a hazy blue-green sea. This coast was all rock, it seemed, from the crests of the mountains to the edge of the water, with little growing from the sparse arid soil.

"There will not be many birds now," Hatiu informed us. "It is not the nesting season."

"That should make things easier," said one of the warriors.

"But no eggs," grumbled another.

Bafa looked up at the cloudless sky. "Let's head down and make camp. We have days of looking for stones ahead of us. And looking at stones," he added, turning his gaze to the rocky landscape about us.

11. Discoveries

A shine among the rocks of a dry stream bed caught my eye. I picked up the stone and wiped the dust from it. "Is this copper?" I asked, holding it up.

Bafa took the shiny pebble and turned it over in his palm. "No, my friend. This is gold."

I did not know the word. "Is it of any value?"

"Many consider it of great value. Marareta told me they used it in that valley you visited." He shrugged. "Here, I suppose its only use would be for ornaments."

"Oh." I looked again at the nugget and recognized it. "Yes, they thought it desirable." I remembered the triangular tokens that could be traded for anything one desired. Even the love of women, which seemed very strange to we who are Mora.

It was the first thing of any value we had found in three days of scouring the hillsides. There was no sign of either stone that went into the making of bronze. "We shall spend tomorrow moving our camp north," our leader told us. "Then we search again."

I feared that none of these men would actually recognize the stone we sought, the gem-like rock that could be made into what Bafa called 'tin.' From time to time, one brought in a piece of quartz — useful enough but not the stone we sought.

As we marched on the morrow, someone pointed to the sea. "A boat!" We all turned to spy a square sail appearing and disappearing in the glare on the water.

"Kohari," said Hatiu, peering at it with eyes shielded by his palms both above and below. "Fishing, I would think. They sometimes seek a catch off these coasts. The waters are rich here."

"As long as they do not land we will not concern ourselves with them," spoke Bafa. "Not that we could do anything while they are out there."

We moved on and found a likely site to encamp. "We would do better to make salt," I told Bafa, only partially in jest, as we rested by a small fire of twigs and brush. "There is always a demand for salt."

"I think we shall leave that to Hei'iro. And to the Kohari. Don't their merchants trade salt to us?"

"They do." I had but learned this on my recent visit to the Great Falls. "I noticed another of these stones you name 'metal' among their wares, heavy and gray. Fishermen use it for weights on their nets."

"Lead? That isn't surprising. It may be the first metal men ever learned to use." Bafa laughed. "And I have not the slightest idea about how it is obtained."

"We were fortunate that the rebels did not know of it. It would make a sling an even more lethal weapon."

Bafa nodded and noted, "That is astute of you, Hito. You ever see the practical applications of things, don't you?" More soberly, he added, "Lord Hareata was slain by a sling-man."

"It was good we had your archers to counter them," I told him. "Some still think the bow a cowardly weapon. A Kohari weapon."

"Killing from afar is one of man's great achievements," said Bafa, with a scornful laugh. "We are much more advanced in the art in my world."

"Then I am glad I do not live there, my lord."

In the morning we again clambered up and down the slopes, seeking copper, seeking tin. All we found were a few more pebbles of gold. "Poyo did say it was gathered here and I think he had no reason to lie," I told our leader. "And I do not think the Kohari would dig for it. The stones must be found on the surface."

"And not very far inland," he replied. "Most likely found by fishermen coming ashore to repair nets or something of the sort." That made sense. The Kohari would not land here specifically to search for these stones.

We would have searched longer but things changed that night. "Where is Fetua?" someone asked. The man was not to be found, so we took torches and searched through the rocks. What was found was his body with no head.

"The Kohari have come ashore," spat Hatiu. "The chance of taking a head or two was too great a temptation." We covered over what remained of Fetua with rocks and returned to our camp.

"They might attack again," I said. "Success makes men bold."

"Too bold, I hope," came Lord Bafa's icy voice, "so I might make them pay for this." This was a Bafa I had not seen in some time, not the pleasant, seemingly carefree person he usually presented to the world. "Douse the fire," he ordered, "and have your weapons at hand."

A short time later we were climbing in the dark, searching for a vantage point from which we might spy our enemy. Would the Kohari be foolish enough to light a fire? Or had they already returned to the sea? We saw nothing in the dark but only sat and waited.

"There," Bafa said, pointing, as the pale light of dawn touched the rocky coast. "Two boats." They were pulled ashore in a little cove below us, slightly to the north.

"They might outnumber us," I cautioned. Even as I looked down on them I was thinking that was a good landing spot. It might be better to visit this coast by sea next time.

Someone laughed. "It does not matter. We are Mora!"

And we were warriors all, men trained in such things.

12. Thoughts

Bafa and his two bowmen rained arrows on the Kohari camp. They did not outnumber us after that. The rest of us charged the bewildered and instantly demoralized enemy. Some fled toward their boats; others stood to fight and were cut down quickly. None escaped.

"All youngsters," spoke Hatiu, looking over the dead. "Probably thought they were going on an adventure."

I looked into the boats. These were no fishermen. There were no nets, only weapons. I pointed this out to Bafa.

"A raiding party out seeking heads?" he mused. "Or a scouting party looking for ways across the mountains? Who can say?

"We must head home immediately," he continued. "Burn these boats." He looked at the dead Kohari. "Throw the bodies onto them first." Soon, two laden, flaming Kohari boats were being pushed out into the water.

And so we turned and marched back across the hills, having accomplished nothing we intended but perhaps having learned something even more valuable. But first, we carried Fetiu's head, found in a woven basket, to place with his body. Rest well, comrade; may you feast with the gods.

The search for metals seemed less urgent now. Arierona would be likely to turn his attention to other more conventional preparations for war. This I assumed; I did not accompany Lord Bafa when he gave his report to the king. I would not return to my life as a warrior here.

Messengers sped off in several directions. To the High King, sure-ly, to important noblemen throughout Arierona's realm, to his neighboring kings. I saw them go as I rested on the banks of A'auwa and thought.

Of many things, I thought. Should I return to Mehetu now? I could offer her little, even if we both desired marriage. Her wealth was slight and mine slighter. It was true that joining the nobility would allow me to serve as a commander of men. It was true that I had no great desire to be one now.

I would do better to go seek fortune, perhaps join those who crossed the hills to trade with the Diwarna. I was known in the Mora trade village there. I had friends. I should see what could be done with my life.

First, I had promised the taona that I would speak with Pana'a. To do so, I could only wait for her to leave her island, when she would. So I sat by A'auwa and thought on things. I seemed to do much of that these days.

Samua came to sit beside me. He smoked an oddly-shaped pipe — I think it was fashioned from a gourd — for some time before speaking. "Pana'a will come over soon. She knows you wait for her."

As priestesses had been coming and going from the isle, I had as-sumed this was so. I would not have asked any of them to tell her I was there. It was nearly evening when the woman paddled to the shore, alone. Ah, she looked much like Rahaita, did she not? I did not know Pana'a well, but had ventured across the mountains with her niece.

She took a seat beside Samua, to the left of both of us. A woman always sits to the left of a group of men. Why, I do not know; it is just how things are done and no one thinks further of it. "I greet the wanderers," she said.

"Greetings to you, Pana'a," I replied. Pana'a is itself a title so there is no need to say 'Lady.' "The Taona Marareta sends his greetings as well. He can not come just now."

"I know, Friend Hito." I was honored to be so addressed. "The Lady Panoha is with child."

Samua spoke. "He told us you foresaw this."

"Perhaps. I foresaw a daughter, eventually. He will name her Rahiri." She sat a while silently, gazing out over A'auwa. Dusk was falling across the wide lake. "That was my name before I became a priestess," she almost whispered.

"He will come," Samua promised. Then, with a boldness that surprised me, he asked, "It is you the taona truly loves, is it not?"

"Once," came the answer. "Once. He will come to me less and less and our love will continue to cool. This is not something I can see, yet I know it." Her voice nearly broke as she said, "And he will never love another as he loved Rahaita."

Pana'a rose. "I have duties in the house of Arierona. We shall speak again on the morrow, my friends."

13. The Priestess

"Out there on the isle, we sought what they called mana. I think that is something like what I knew as 'grace' when I was in another world."

"I do not know that word," replied Pana'a. "That's enough breakfast for me." She reclined on one elbow and watched the two of us continue our meal.

"Mana may be found in many ways," I said, though I felt foolish explaining such things in front of a priestess. "Through war. Even through making love."

Samua chuckled. "I suppose those are sacraments of a sort. You don't know that word either, but I'm sure there is a proper term in your convoluted Mora tongue."

Pana'a nodded. "Undoubtedly. Our friend Marareta once suggested to me that language that is too precise may lead its speakers into rigid ways of thought. He prefers to speak of such things in the trade pidgin rather than the Mora tongue."

"They devoted themselves to one god out there," Samua said, returning to his original thought. "The overarching Sky. That was what attracted me to them. That is like the God I knew." For a moment, he gathered the words to explain this. "You see, they call him Rai here, but it's the same idea, isn't it? The Father of All."

"A small god is good enough for me," was my opinion. "Like Teva whom the Taona Marareta has chosen to follow."

"But is this Teva even real?" asked Samua. "Does he exist anywhere other than in men's heads?" I had wondered such things about the gods myself, but spoke not of them. I suspected it did not truly matter.

"Amid the infinite worlds, Teva not only can exist but Teva must exist. A powerful wizard such as your friend Oorto might be able to seek him out. But he shouldn't." Pana'a sounded quite sure of that. "We call our goddess Marahina, Moon Woman, but we do not know her name. Perhaps the true names of all the gods are hidden and we humans have but given them titles we make up."

"We give ourselves names, too," I pointed out. "Or our parents do. It makes us no more or less who we are."

"Most true, Hito. Or would you prefer a different name?" Pana'a smiled at her own little jest.

"I might like to add 'Ari' to it." That is, to be a nobleman.

Both smiled at that. "You are sometimes quite the traditionalist," stated Samua.

Pana'a shook her head. "Our Hito may be conservative by nature, but he is no traditionalist."

"Marareta once called him a skeptic," said Samua.

"This may be so," I agreed. "I am a practical man. But I have been also an ambitious man and a self-centered one, at times."

"You have changed," Pana'a observed. "Not completely but you have begun a new journey, a different journey."

"I think it began with crossing the mountains. And then the death of the Lady Rahaita." Yes, Marareta was not the only one set on a new path that day. I asked Pana'a, "Is it true that you saw what would happen? Could not you have changed it or warned her?"

"It is so. I saw Rahaita lying slain but knew not how it would come to be." There was great sadness, great weariness in the voice of the priestess. "We of the Sacred Isle thought perhaps we could hide her, keep her from her fate, but should have known better. Our visions are always true."

I asked then, "Do you have any visions for me, Pana'a?"

"None, Hito, but I believe you will find what you seek. You must trust in yourself." She rose. "I think too that you should speak with the priest Hoka. Marareta prizes his words."

"I've heard enough of the old windbag myself," stated Samua.

"And he of you, Samua," came Pana'a's retort. "I shall be leaving at the mid-morning, Hito. You may cross A'auwa with me, if you wish."

"You intend to leave us soon, don't you?" Samua asked after the priestess departed. "It could do you well to talk with old Hoka," he admitted.

"Yes, I'm going to try my hand at being a trader. I have not yet decided on my wares." I had been pondering at some length what I might carry with me to the lands of the Diwarna.

"Bark cloth, maybe?" he suggested. "It's light, anyway!"

"My trip across the hills got me thinking of salt," I said. "But I've no doubt there are those selling that already." Samua nodded and decided to have another yam. I continued as he unpeeled it. "Maybe your cloth isn't a bad idea." It was many seasons since I was last in the trade village. I tried to recall what the Mora merchants there had offered. Rope. Baskets. Carved wooden bowls. Bone needles. These I remembered.

Well, I would come up with something. I'd best prepare to accompany the Priestess of the Moon.

14. A Shrine

Only the strokes of our paddles disturbed the surface of A'auwa on this still morning. A few high clouds were beginning to gather to the northwest, a portent of possible rain later, tonight, perhaps, or tomorrow. Now, the sun blazed without mercy on us. From time to time, I scooped up a handful of water to splash on my head.

"It should be cool beneath the trees at Teva's shrine," Pana'a assured me. "Cooler than elsewhere."

"Cooler than your isle?"

"That you may never know, Hito, without losing your life as a price." I knew well her island was forbidden to men. Crushing was the traditional penalty and Arierona honored tradition.

"Hoka may have something useful to say to you. If not, his wine and his company are always pleasant." We passed surprisingly close by the Sacred Island now, closer than I had ever seen it and larger than I had realized. It made me uncomfortable.

High rocky flanks stood forbiddingly, mirrored in the water. Trees did grow on the isle, some of them quite tall, so at least there was shade for the women who dwelt there. A landing place, I knew, was located on the far side but we would not go there!

Then we were past and angling southeastward, still distant from the far shores of A'auwa. There was forest by the lake down there, old trees that were now protected as a sacred place. Within those trees lay shrines to several gods, including that of Teva, where old Hoka dwelt with his wives.

We reached his little hut around noon. Fortunately, Hoka had not begun his siesta. I was unsure whether our presence would keep him from napping anyway. He offered us wine, wine he made from whatever fruit was available at the season, and we sat on the bench before his abode. Both wives rested nearby, neither particularly young but definitely not as old as Hoka.

Old also was the wooden statue of Teva that stood closer to the roadway through the forest. A mossy log lay beside it on which one could rest. Both could bear replacing. A few chickens scratched around the hut, red and gold feathers flashing when a bit of sunlight found its way through the leaves.

"You seek even as your master did," spoke the ancient priest. A bit of purple wine that had dribbled onto his pot belly was attracting flies. "I told Marareta he was not meant to hide away in a shrine, even though he yearned for its peace. Of you, I am not so sure."

"I certainly have no desire to be a priest of Teva," I countered. "Yet I do seek a direction."

"Many serve Teva in one fashion or another," he informed me.

"Why follow Teva rather than Longo?" I asked. "Isn't Longo the god of love?" And Teva was a bringer of rain. How did that fit in?

"Longo is the god of sex," he said, "a god of power. Teva is a god of love and of the home. A god of fertility."

Pana'a added her words to his. "Just as Tu and Te'eta are both gods of war. But Te'eta is all about blood lust and battle where Tu overlooks the making of war. He is as much the god of politics."

"Even so," agreed Hoka, taking another swig from his wine-bowl. "Yet very different."

Both the priestess and I had to laugh at that. Other laughter arose behind us, where stood two more priestesses of the isle.

"We saw you paddling across," said one. "And we saw this handsome warrior with you." Both gave me a thorough looking over.

"So we followed," spoke the other.

"You are always welcome here, my girls," said Hoka, though perhaps neither was exactly a girl. But they were not old, and good enough to look upon. I supposed, as Pana'a, they had gifts of prophecy, not so powerful as hers but there none the less.

Pana'a did not reprove them, though I believe she was annoyed. The priestesses on a whole tended to be quite independent. I remembered this of them. "Perhaps you will learn something," she told them.

One giggled. "That is what we hoped!"

"They are not usually so silly," Pana'a assured me. They were putting it on for my sake. I could see that. But I was here to learn from Hoka.

Maybe later there would be time for other lessons.

"So you are going to seek your fortune in the north?" asked Hoka, turning his attention back to me. If his glance occasionally strayed to the priestesses, I certainly couldn't blame him. My own did, as well.

"And more than my fortune, sir. A direction."

"There are an infinite number of directions you could turn this very moment," he told me and then noted Pana'a. "Our priestess would correct me but is too polite. Not truly infinite, I'll admit, but an exceptionally large number."

"We are bound by the finite universe in which we dwell, Holy One," she replied. "I am not sure even the gods have infinite choices."

"Yes, I know. Except the One, if such actually exists. Such questions are one reason I drink wine." He took another sip. "It is getting near nap time, you know."

He turned his eyes back to me. I'm not sure he was quite able to focus them. "You will not find peace beyond the hills. I can tell you this now and I do not have the gifts of Pana'a! But you may find many other things, so go and look. But know the things you need may be right here when you return, right where you left them."

Mehetu, maybe? Or something else entirely.

"You would have an affinity for Teva. I can feel this. The Taona Marareta stumbled into his priesthood and that was good, perhaps even fated —" He glanced again at Pana'a. "Yes, my dear, I know you do not believe in fate. Anyway, Marareta could serve Teva but had no need to do so. You, my friend, may find such a need within you."

"And we could help you find it," offered one of the priestesses.

"Or something else," said the other.

I shook my head. "I could not see living the life you do, Master Hoka." But I lied. I could see myself here but did not wish to admit it. A god of love and peace and gentle rain would not be worst of masters.

When I looked again to the priest he had dozed off. I and all three priestesses sat and talked for a time of nothing in particular and we walked by A'auwa, talking of nothing at all, before sharing a late afternoon meal with the refreshed holy man and his spouses. It was near dusk when Pana'a and I launched her canoe onto the lake.

And it was dark by the time we reached the other side of A'auwa. In the stillness of the night, Pana'a asked, "Is my son well?"

"He is, Pana'a, and loved. I am sure Marareta will bring him back here soon."

"Yes, he will. But could I bear to look upon him? Rahaita became his mother in name and now Panoha is his mother in fact." For a time, the only sound was the lake lapping at the shore. "Maratoa will share in my gifts, the gifts that killed both Rahaita and my sister. This I have seen but more I can not say."

I stepped out onto the shore and Pana'a turned and paddled toward her isle, disappearing into night.

15. Setting Forth

If one of the priestesses found her way to my sleeping chamber later, I am not to be blamed. We both knew there would be no entanglements for us, she pledged to serve her goddess, I to be leaving soon. I did wonder what became of the other one. Maybe they threw dice and she lost.

I had come up with an idea for the wares I would traffic across the hills and must see about obtaining them. I was not wealthy and had little left when I was finished. I would also carry other sundries, more conventional trade goods, to fill up my pack. It would be a heavy load and a great distance. The life of a trader is not so easy!

Were the way less rugged, one might drag a load behind one on skids or, better, use one of those new rolling baskets — I know not a better name for them — that Dutsa was building at the trade village. But a commodious basket strapped to my back was the only option I had.

Beka arrived before my departure date, Palala on his shoulder, and then left almost as soon, off to his parents' house where Miruhata and E'eva, his wife and that of Poneiva, waited. There too was their little sister, Teme, the heroic young woman who had slain Hara'a. When I spoke of women who matched Bafa with the bow, I was thinking of Teme — though also of Amirea, wife of Aranu. She might be the best of them all, when facing a straw target, but had not a heart made for war.

The women, I understood, missed not being the ones who cared for little Maratoa, son of Marareta, now that he lived in his father's house. But they would get over it; both had children of their own on the way. Soon they would all move to the house of the High King.

I was surprised when Arierona himself came to see me, Lord Aranu at his side. The king made a last attempt to keep me in his service. I suspect that Aranu asked it of him.

"There are many noble widows among my relatives," spoke King Arierona. "Take one to wife and you would have a place among my captains."

"It is a place I no longer desire, my lord. I shall be a warrior no more."

"A trader instead? That is not an easy life."

"Yet, my lord, I must search elsewhere for my place." I smiled and added, "Perhaps I shall search for Lord Bafa's stones while I am there."

"Then I must see that he speaks with you before you leave."

Aranu grinned. "Bafa probably wishes he were going along." To me he said, "My new second seems a good man. He worries too much about me, however."

"I told him to do so, my lord."

Aranu might not have seen the humor in that but Arierona did. The wisdom of it too, I think. The king wished me luck and the favor of the gods and we made our farewell. It would be long before I saw Arierona again, or Aranu.

All that was left was to visit the net makers. There were several who lived and worked by A'auwa and it was their work I would carry to the Diwarna. I had made sure to bring some of those lead weights brought by the Kohari. The craftsmen greatly appreciated those and wanted more. Had I not intended to head north, I could have made a business of bringing those up from the Great Falls!

One thing I knew was that Diwarna fishermen employed only a sort of basket and had no nets. If I could convince them to use these instead, I could have a ready market and the net-makers of A'auwa to supply it.

But that is getting far ahead of myself, is it not?

Six nets I stuffed into my pack, each within nested woven baskets which themselves might also be sold. I am afraid the weights made them far heavier than they otherwise would have been. Around them, the bark cloth and, finally, bits of jewelry tucked away. All this recent interest in stones and pebbles of gold had turned my mind in this direction. There are always those who will desire pretty baubles.

In the gray of before-dawn I set forth, only Samua there to see me off. I hoped that he, too, would find success in his searches.

Part II. The Trader

16. *The House of Isa*

"I thought you might be here, Master Ulani."

"There is too much turmoil in the house of the High King right now," replied the slender young man. His dark face spoke of his half-Diwarna heritage. "I shall go back to Poneiva when he finishes building!"

"Who is that?" came a voice from within the hut. It was a rich voice, a voice trained in the art of telling tales. The Taona Isa, it would be, the man who had taught Ulani. He came forth. "Ah, the warrior Hito. Your large friend is not with you?"

He meant Aranu. "He remains with Arierona, Master," I replied. "I no longer serve the king." I lowered my heavy pack to the dock. "I am a trader now."

"Honest work," allowed the old man. "Better than being a priest." Isa had a dislike for religion, though he counted Marareta among his friends. "Come, Rania," he called, "we have a guest!"

The house of Isa was not so distant from where I had begun my journey, a short way down the Teoma and then up one of the many tributary streams. It was a good place to turn away from the river and start toward the still-distant lands of the Diwarna. I had come by canoe this time. No swimming across rivers with a pack-basket full of trade goods!

"Why are you standing out here?" scolded his wife as she joined us. "Come in and drink my husband's beer." Rania was somewhat younger than the master storyteller though, to be honest, Isa was not truly that old, perhaps six tens of years, and vigorous.

The hut was as remembered, more than spacious enough for the couple and a servant. Not the same servant as before, but a different young woman. All this was provided to Isa by the High King and the two High Kings before him, the hut and anything else he needed. More than he needed, Isa was inclined to grumble, not that he turned any of it away.

Once I dulled the edge of the knife known as hunger, I said to Ulani, "Speaking of turmoil in the High King's house, your mother is there now." That was the Lady Pua who had adopted young Ulani so he might be accepted as a man of the Mora. It also ennobled him, not that he cared — becoming a master storyteller would be high rank in itself.

"She has left the house of Marareta?"

"For a time." Then I must need fill them in on all the gossip of that house, including Panoha's pregnancy. "I met a lad there, the son of Hareata who should study with a master such as you." I had been looking at Isa when I said this, but then turned my gaze to Ulani. "Or you."

Ulani nodded thoughtfully. "His mother's love for the old tales is well known, and her patronage of those who tell them."

The older poet said only, "Let him come when he is ready," and belched.

"How far do you travel?" asked Ulani.

"At least as far as the trade village where once you lived. Beyond that, I do not know." I laughed. "I might go all the way across the mountains!" That thought was always with me.

Ulani shook his head at that. "You would never return, my friend. You need not go into exile."

"I only seek the stones that Lord Bafa desires for the making of weapons. It might be needed to go to the mountains for those."

"But not cross them," said Isa. "That would be too far to bring them back."

I nodded. "This is true. The nearer, the better."

Rania spoke. "Is there not an epic, my husband, about Mora who went into exile?"

"Yes, those who opposed the first High King, Uiri. You remember it, don't you Ulani?"

"I do, Master." He turned to me. "There are many tales of those wars. Very long tales!"

"Start with the part about the exiles," ordered the Taona Isa. To him, I am sure, Ulani would always be an apprentice.

The young storyteller began:

At the cliffs they stood defeated,
yet defiant still, the warriors.
Shall we leap? the women asked them,
Shall we give ourselves to Wanga?

It went on like this for far too long but, in time, those who opposed the first High King, those who followed the ancient ways, had taken to canoes below the Great Falls — for that was their last stronghold — and sailed away. Where they went, the poem did not say, but rather went on to speak of those who were victorious in that war. Epics ever favor the winner.

When he finished, I remarked, "The Lord Hareata feared he might need to flee into exile if we lost our war against the rebels. He and Temani'itu stood ready to sail away with their kin and followers."

Isa nodded. "It is fortunate that was not needed. Though Hareata left us anyway." He bowed his head a moment in respect, as did we all. "Some tales say the Mora who fled settled among the Kohari and even became lords over those people. I do not know."

"The rebels are all beaten now?" asked Rania.

"They are," I replied. "There are a few bands still roaming the north but they are without leaders or direction."

Ulani said, "Now, I think there is more to be feared from Poneiva's cousins than from those rebels. Some more closely related to my late brother Ve'eta feel one of them should have been chosen High King." I did not know this; Ulani was far closer to the goings on around Poneiva than I.

"I shall not pass close to the High King's home on my way across the hills," I said. Of Isa, I asked, "Might I leave my canoe here? I think it best I use my legs the rest of the way."

"Only if you promise to return," he told me.

17. A Meeting

All the rivers I crossed now should be shallow enough to wade, even the Teiri when I reached it. That would be somewhere to the east of the village of Marihana, where many traders began their journey on the road across the hills. I would meet that road further north.

It was on my third day from leaving Isa's house, traversing ever rising land that was beginning to change from farm and forest to grassy savanna, that my path converged with another. I could see a distant traveler trudging along it, a large man, it seemed, coming from a more westerly direction.

I might as well wait and greet him, I thought, and rest. Travel was slow with my heavy pack and he would have caught up anyway, in time.

Which first recognized the other, I know not. Taki. Would he see me as an enemy? And why was he here, so far from the house of Marareta? I stood ready for action, if need be. But no, the man greeted me with a grin. "So, we walk the same road," he said. "In more ways than one!"

"I greet you, Taki," I spoke, warily. "Though it is unexpected."

He shrugged. "The taona asked I leave his service." He seemed to be surprisingly good natured about it. "He wanted Mehetu for himself, I am sure, and was jealous of me." He peered at me. "Maybe of you too?"

I would certainly not tell him I had a part in this. "Ah, then we have both lost our chance."

"Why would she have wanted a commoner such as you? At least I am of noble birth," he proclaimed. "Where do you travel, little man?"

I took no offense to his naming me so. He knew this little man could put his face in the dirt. "I cross the hills to trade with the Diwarna. It is time I thought of seeking wealth rather than honor." I reached down and patted the heavily-laden pack-basket I had been carrying.

Taki nodded but I think he disapproved of this as something a warrior should be doing. "I seek to join the service of some lord here in the north," he told me.

"Best you not look for a place among the men of Anana. Young Toare is unlikely to put in a good word for you."

"I know." He frowned, his heavy eyebrows almost coming together. "That is my own fault. I make for the house of Mahutunoa. If I find no one willing to take me on there, I will journey on to Naire or maybe even Ruapata. At least I can partake of their hospitality!"

"Many warriors were lost in those kingdoms during the wars. There should be nobles with a place for a man such as you." I chuckled. "Widows, too, and younger than Mehetu."

"Then maybe the taona did me a favor. The Lord Marareta was not unkind to me and presented gifts to make the parting easier. It was not something he needed to do."

We both gathered our things and began to trudge north. This was a well-marked trail, a much-traveled one. It would lead to the house of Mahutunoa but I would turn from it before then.

"I have heard of that club you carry." Taki peered at the short bronze sword that hung at my side. "Some say you brought it from the land of the gods."

He sounded doubtful; I would have been, too, if told such a story. "It came from a land beyond the mountains," I told him, "but the gods do not live there. Only men." That there were powerful sorcerers among those men I felt no need to mention.

"Men like us? Or Kohari?"

That seemed a sensible question. Strangely, none had before asked it of me. "Like the Diwarna," I said, "but with far greater knowledge than those we know here."

"Hmm. I have not known many Diwarna."

"They prefer not to leave their own lands."

We walked on the rest of that day, becoming surprisingly comradely, considering that we probably did not like each other very much. There were many tales we could tell to pass the time, and Taki had an unsuspected knowledge of songs.

That he blustered to protect himself was obvious. There was not so much of that here, with only the two of us. Given a crowd, I was sure the braggart, the bully, would reappear. That must be as it would be, and could be of no concern of mine.

I would not be Taki's spiritual adviser. I would not step into the role of priest.

18. Bodyguard

Two days we accompanied each other on that road, and two nights we camped together, cold camps for there was no firewood readily at hand and we were too weary to go searching any out. We set no watch. Was not our nation now at peace?

Something woke me. Ah, Taki's snoring. I looked up to a thin moon, appearing and disappearing amid scuttling clouds. There was little light to cast shadows, but did I not see shadows moving just beyond our camp?

Perhaps it was not my comrade's noisy breathing that had brought me out of sleep. Perhaps I had sensed something else. I shook him awake. "Trouble," I whispered.

The man immediately grasped his great stone ax. I carried few weapons but Taki had the full equipment of a warrior. My sword was barely in my hand when they charged.

There were four or five of them. I am not sure. Spears, they had, and at least one club. The remnants of some rebel band? It seemed likely. And good warriors, too, not unskilled peasants.

But not as good as we were. I knew my business and Taki, even if a poor wrestler, could handle his weapons. I do not think our attackers expected this. Certainly not a giant wielding a heavy ax.

Nor my blade. Using a sword was not unlike fighting with the traditional Mora war club, but its edge was sharper than any piece of hard wood or polished stone. I know it cut into my first opponent, who shrieked and backed off. The second man to rush in slid off the blade a moment later, his life blood gushing from a gaping wound in his abdomen, and from mouth and nose.

Then they were gone. "I do not think they will come back," spoke Taki. I agreed. A man lay at his feet, his head crushed.

Taki looked down at him for a moment and then away. "I give thanks to Babi," he murmured so I might barely hear him. Was Taki embarrassed to follow a goddess rather than some masculine, warlike divinity? There was certainly no wrong in honoring the Earth, the Mother of All.

I should offer a prayer myself. What god I might thank, I had no idea. Perhaps the one Taki honored — had the big man not been with me, I would surely be dead. Dawn was beginning to show the world around us, a world with no men other than the two of us.

"Should we bury them?" wondered Taki.

I would not have, this I admit, but many a warrior would disapprove. The sun and the wind and the vultures would have taken care of things, in their own way, in their own time. Before I might decide on an answer, I spied men in the distance.

My traveling companion looked where I pointed. "More trouble?"

"If it is, it is more than we can handle," I replied. They were a dozen men or more. Warriors, I could see, as they drew closer.

They ringed us about on reaching us, their leader coming to peer at the two bodies. Satisfied, he nodded and called to his men. "It is well." They came in to get a look themselves.

"We have been tracking these men," spoke the commander of the troop. "They would attack traders on the road and take their wares." He gave us a closer look. "You are warriors?"

"I am," replied Taki. "I have come north seeking a place."

"I am only a trader, my lord," I told him. There was no need to let these men know anything more of me.

The man laughed. "You did well in choosing your bodyguard, Trader!" To Taki he said, "Come to the house of Mahutunoa. We can use men like you."

He turned his eyes again to the two bodies on the ground. "Bury this carrion before we move on," he ordered his warriors.

They paid us no more attention so we gathered our belongings and traveled onward. Taki gave me more than one curious look but said naught. On the next day we parted, he heading on to the king's house, I angling northwest toward the road over the hills. There were few words in that parting.

On the road, when I reached it, were other traders, some of them men I knew, and I joined a group. Many traders had I met while I stayed at the trade village across the hills, when first returned from the mountains. There with Marareta and Rika and Rahaita and all my comrades I had rested for a while.

Soon we climbed to the gap through those hills, to stand gazing northward into the lands of the Diwarna.

19. Pots

I knew that I must speak to Gordie. To sell my nets to the Diwarna, I must go to them, show them how they worked in use. It would do no good to demonstrate them in this little village in the middle of a dry savanna.

Oh, I could sell them directly to Gordie, I supposed, and he would carry them to the jungle and swamp. Surely he would be interested. Either way, as I said, I must speak to the man.

It was little more than three years ago when he and the others from the sea had come to our world, and Gordie hardly more than a boy at the time. Now, he was practically a king, controlling much of the trade that came south from the Gurang valley to this village. He was beginning to overshadow the Mora who supposedly ran things here. Our recent civil wars had helped facilitate this.

Indeed, he could have thrown out the Mora representative and taken control, for the High King was far away. I am sure Gordie knew things would run more smoothly if left as they were.

But he was not at the village, nor was his wife, Demba. Poa'ave, 'Black Pearl,' Ulani had named her and my people had come to call her. A woman of the Diwarna, she was sister to my comrade in journey, the wizard Oorto. I understood she had a child now but had not heard the name chosen.

Many others I knew were here. Ma'are and her husband, Heho, onetime courier for the High King, ran things for the Mora and lived in the house where Lady Pua once dwelt. Marareta had first met the lady there, I had heard, and made love to her as well. I had not asked him of this but can believe it.

And there were the cats. Only two, Kaleea and Ulap, had we brought back from the Valley of Visions, but now many cats resided in the trade village. Soon, someone would carry them over the hills and the lands of the Mora would be overrun as well.

I laid my wares out with those of the other traders, my first morning in the village, the cloth, the jewelry, the baskets. The nets I did not display but did not hide them either, placing them behind me where I sat. They might catch someone's interest. One of Dutsa's wheeled baskets — barrows, he named them — rolled past, loaded with freshly dug yams. Why had no one taken a barrow back to Mora lands? Surely one could sell as many as one had.

In time. Things were settling down and trade returning to normal after the war. "I like these," a voice murmured. It was Tala, looking over the ornaments. The shy half-Diwarna woman had become somewhat wealthy, by the standards of this place, as she and her friend Amlee had introduced pottery-making skills learned beyond the mountains.

"I greet you, Tala," I said. "Is your husband about?"

She shook her head. "He is not my man anymore. I wanted to stay here and make pots." Her eyes lifted and gazed eastward. I understood this; he had been one of those who chose to settle in a secluded valley there, a place where half-breeds such as he could have a home.

I understood also that Gordie had recruited some of those men, men who had crossed the mountains with me, and others like them, as his personal retainers. That was wise; they were not Mora nor Diwarana nor Kohari and so had no loyalties save to him.

That mattered little to me at the moment. "Surely you have many new suitors," I told her. She blushed, obvious even with her dark skin. "I am always willing to trade for some of your fine pots," I continued. I had no great desire to take any back with me but they could be exchanged with other traders.

"There were pretty things, um, over there," Tala said. "Made of sun-stone." That was what the Kohari called copper. Yes, there was good jewelry made in the Valley. A fair amount had been worn by those of us who returned.

"I would like to find a place where one can dig sun-stone from the ground," I said. "Have you seen any?" She only shook her head. Then on a whim, I asked, "What about *rus*?" This was the name for gold in the land across the mountains. Maybe it could be translated as 'dawn-stone.'

"Oh, yes, Hito. We find it in the streams sometime. But we are looking for clay, not those pebbles!"

So, gold again. Not the metal for which I sought but perhaps useful anyway. "It can make nice jewelry," I noted. "I might be willing to trade for some."

But I could not make jewelry. I would have to find someone who could, here or in the Mora homeland. Being a trader was complicated. I did end up with a couple pots and less jewelry a short time later — my first transaction as a trader.

In time, I had mats and crocodile skins — not the best ones — traded to me for my cloth and baskets, and many questions about the nets that I had placed further back, away from the wares I offered. Once people knew what they were, their interest waned.

Had I made a mistake with those?

Heho came by eventually, his usual cheerful self, but grown a bit fat now that he no longer traversed the Mora realm, carrying other men's words. "Come and eat with Ma'are and me this evening," he said, "and meet our children."

"Children?" I had known Ma'are was pregnant when last I was here.

"A boy and a girl," he replied. "I sometimes think we should go where they can grow up with other Mora." He looked around. "But I like it here, away from the center of things."

"The center of things may call your wife back to it, one of these days." Ma'are came of an important noble family. Poneiva would not forget she was here. Changing the subject, I asked, "Would you expect Gordie to show up any time soon?"

"I would. He likes to keep an eye on us."

20. Gordie

I admit that there was another motive in going to the Diwarna, beyond selling them a few nets. It would allow me to continue my search for the stones I desired, to perhaps go part of the way up the Gurang, as I had with Marareta two years before. It seemed a good place to approach the mountains.

Maybe I was just searching for whatever I could find, truly. Coming this far only to sit in the trade village seemed pointless.

When I went to the house of — ah, let us call it the house of the Mora — that evening, I found that Gordie had arrived. He did not look like an important man, this pale, slight youth dressed in a Diwarna apron.

It was the Diwarna who gave him his power here, not the warriors he now commanded. He had shown them that they had the upper hand in this place, that they were the reason men came to trade, that they could be in control of that trade. Not that the tribes who roamed the Diwarna realm cared that much, you understand, but they saw reason in his words and let him gradually take greater control of what went south to the trade village.

That he truly liked his wife's people and wanted to help them did not hurt. Demba was not with him on this visit.

Yet as soon as he saw me, he said, "You must come to my home. Demba and Oorto would love to have you there." I had no doubt that Gordie had heard of my nets and already knew I wished to go. Even before I became a trader I had enough sense not to say such things aloud.

There was much to speak of, gossip of all his friends among the Mora, as we sat upon the high porch, eating and watching the market slowly wind down at the approach of night. In time, the talk turned to Bafa.

"I am sure," I told Gordie, "that you have heard I am interested in certain stones." He nodded an agreement. "It is for Bafa that I seek them." For the most part this was so, though I hoped to get something from it. Or maybe I was just searching for the sake of searching, to have something worth doing. I was not completely sure.

"He's looking to make bronze. I've heard this." He asked then, "You can recognize this Cassiwhatzit?"

"I can. I think I shall call it star-stone, since some Kohari say it is sacred to the Morning Star."

"Sounds good to me. I wish you had brought some so I could get a look."

"If I find any, I shall be sure to show it you."

That brought a laugh. "But not where you found it, maybe?" Gordie reflected a moment before going on. "It would be far to carry your stones back to the Mora. If you found them, it would be more sensible to make the bronze here, or at least refine the one metal or the other." Those who sat with us did not understand our words but I had seen this done. Gordie made sense.

"I shall be about this place all of tomorrow," he went on. "There are things to which I must attend. But I leave the next day if you wish to accompany me to the Gurang." Without waiting for an answer, he turned to our hosts. "My honey-hunters should be arriving in a day or two. As always, you are welcome to as much of their wares as you might need."

"We thank you, Gordie," replied Ma'are. "We could not continue to feed so many without your gifts."

The young man said only, "It is needful to keep this place working smoothly."

"Sometimes I think you are the true Hero from the Sea," remarked Heho. "Certainly to those who dwell here." He turned to me. "This village would have been deserted while war raged across the hills, were it not for Gordie."

"That too was needful."

"In his own way," I said, "I think Gordie sees the future as well as his wife's brother."

"Better," replied Gordie, with a laugh.

21. Swamps

"The Kohari name your dawn-stone *windu*," Gordie told me. "What was the word you used for it?"

"Rus," I told him. "It means something like 'dawn's glow' in Zikem, the language of the Valley." I gave the man a sidelong look. "You have dealings with the Kohari?"

"Traders do sometimes come up the Gurang. Mostly those who seek to fell trees. You know of that." I did. Many of the Mora's sea-going canoes were constructed of logs floated down to the Great Falls by Kohari. "I know not to trust them too much," he added. That, I thought, was a good idea both when dealing with Kohari and with traders.

I had not followed this path before, not when I joined Marareta in his pursuit of Nezama. We had traveled further east, toward the upper reaches of the great Gurang River where it tumbled down from the mountains. We walked beside the little stream that arose from the spring at the trade village — that spring was the reason the village stood where it did. In time, it was joined by other streams, all flowing toward the still-distant Gurang.

Only one other man accompanied us, a taciturn warrior of mixed heritage. I would hazard his mother was Kohari; this meant he had no place in Mora society, where status is inherited through the maternal line. My friend Heho was half-Kohari but his mother was Mora, a woman who wed a freed slave. Therefor, he was considered Mora and no one thought any further of it.

"Most of the Kohari copper, I understand," he went on, "is found as nuggets that come down from mountain streams. There must be more of it up there somewhere."

"But one might wander the mountains for a lifetime and not find it," I replied. "They are very large."

"I would certainly never attempt to climb over them as you did, Friend Hito!"

"I would have followed Marareta anywhere," was my answer and the truth.

"Yes. Many would." Whether Gordie was among them, I do not know.

We reached a spot where we could take to the water eventually, a place where several canoes were pulled up onto the sand to await their owners. Or any who had need — the Diwarna were not possessive of their belongings. The stream had become a small river, shallow and sandy-bottomed. I spied my first crocodile soon thereafter, but it was small and one that dined on fish, such as are found in the rivers of my own homeland. Great man-eaters lurked in the Gurang, I had heard.

"Do we go to the village, sir?" asked our attendant. I was not sure what status or title these people accorded to Gordie, but they were definitely respectful.

"Yes, first," he answered. "Then, Hito," he continued, "you must come to the house of Gordie."

Our way gradually became swampland, the edges of the stream disappearing among the trees. When exactly we left that stream and entered the swamp itself I am not certain, but at some point I did realize we had done so. "My master must steer now," the warrior said to me in a low voice. "I have been here many times but still can not find the way." He looked respectfully toward Gordie. "He knows the swamps as well as those born here."

I certainly would have been just as lost as Gordie's retainer. There seemed no landmarks here, just water and the mighty cypress trees. Yet we came around one of those cypress and beheld a rambling group of huts on high pilings. The pilings looked rather spindly to my eye. I was not sure I would trust myself up there!

"This is the village where Marareta first met Poneiva," Gordie told me. "I was not with him then. Nesmith — Nezama — had us out rowing on the river." He secured our canoe to the bamboo dock. "It is the largest of the Diwarna villages, a center for all those who dwell in the swamps. So here I do much of my business."

"Is your wife here?" I asked.

"I doubt it. But her brother might be." With that, he clambered up the ladder. By the time we followed, he was in conference with a group of Diwarna.

"He will be busy until dark. After dark, too, maybe," said my companion. "We had best amuse ourselves."

I looked around. There seemed little to do. Perhaps I should go down and get one of my nets. If I started casting from the dock it would surely attract attention.

But no. It would be best not to get ahead of Gordie and whatever plans he had. "There is food," said the warrior. "We may help ourselves." He gestured toward bowls and baskets arrayed about a fire smoldering on a packed clay floor. "They keep those smoking day and night to keep the insects away." He slapped at one that bit him at that moment and laughed.

"I call myself Pahe," said the man, as we seated ourselves. A word from the Kohari — 'bitter' it meant. I wondered if his mother had named him so or he chose it himself. "We seem to be the only visitors today. Sometimes your people come up the Gurang to trade, but the way is kept secret and a Diwarna must guide them here." He bit into some thick-rinded fruit I did not recognize, with pink flesh and many seeds inside. "The Kohari would make short work of this place if they could find it."

22. The Stone House

"It seems Oorto is with his sister at my house," announced Gordie. "That is a bit unusual. He usually divides his time between this village and the one of his birth. Doing shaman things, you know." We had not seen Gordie since arriving the previous day.

"Are we going to leave?" I asked.

"No, first you must show these people your nets. That is why you came, is it not?"

It was. So I went down onto the dock and retrieved one from our canoe. One could leave anything anywhere among the Diwarna; the very idea of theft was foreign to them.

It was but a simple cast-net, the sort common among my people. The lead weights were an innovation of sorts, certainly an improvement over tying rocks into the lines, but the whole idea of such a net was new to these Diwarna. I cast a few times from the dock, demonstrating how it worked. There were few fish in that water but they got the idea.

When I finished, the net was passed from hand to hand and there was a great deal of discussion. I have no understanding of Diwarna — few outsiders ever learn that complicated language — but they seemed to be impressed. "Leave that one here," said Gordie. "I'll tell them it is a gift. Fear not, you will be compensated. In fact," he seemed to suddenly decide, "I think I shall buy all your nets from you."

This was agreeable to me. I might or might not wish to bring more nets to trade someday. There would always be some demand, I suspected. Moreover, the fibers from which they were made grew in Mora lands, not here, though undoubtedly some Diwarna would attempt to duplicate one.

Gordie conferred with the knot of Diwarna for a moment, speaking their tongue as though he were born to it. "They thank you," he reported, returning to us. "What say we get on our way?"

I was willing. Into the canoe we climbed and headed off in some direction. Ask me not which! After a time, I realized we were once again in more swiftly flowing water, edging into a stream of some sort. Then we were in the open. I suspected this was the same little river we had left the previous day. "Ah," said Pahe. I think he recognized where he was. That is a good feeling.

"The house is but a short distance downstream," called Gordie. "It will be to our right."

And so it was. It looked little like the houses of the Mora, for it was built not with strong timbers but with walls of stone. On a rise by this stream it stood, on solid ground, rocky ground.

"It's a half-day journey yet down to the Gurang from here," he announced. "I'm more interested in traveling the other direction, most of the time." We steered in to a sandy beach and pulled the canoe up beside several others. "I'll put a dock here, in time."

This was more than a house. Gordie was building a village of his own here, a compound such as any great noble might have, with outbuildings, and with gardens lying about it. On drawing closer to the house, I saw that it actually was of the familiar post and beam build, but with stones between instead of mats of grass or palm frond — not the supporting walls of fitted stone I had seen on the other side of the mountains. But the idea was the same — defense.

I stood looking at it all for a moment. "Shall we start calling you King Gordie?"

"Best not," came a familiar man's voice. "He is already too full of himself."

There was a snicker. "That is so," agreed a woman. Demba and Oorto, and in Demba's arms, a child. "Her name is Malee," said her mother, and giggled again. "She is another reason Gordie is full of himself." Demba remained a handsome girl — woman, I should say. Her hair fell in black waves on either side of her strong cheekbones.

"And rightly so," said the girl's father, giving his wife a kiss, and then another for the child. The pair were little more than children themselves, yet Gordie was, indeed, almost a king.

"It is good to see you, Friend Hito," spoke Oorto. "It has been long."

A year? No, longer. We slowly mounted the steps and entered the house of Gordie. There was much to talk of with my old friend.

I had barely realized Gordie had disappeared before he returned to us. He had doffed his Diwarna apron of woven grasses in favor of a kilt of bark cloth. I had noted already that Demba dressed similarly.

"I dress as a Diwarna tribesman when I do business. My people here need to see me as one of them."

'His' people? Gordie saw my expression.

"Yes, my people. I became Diwarna when I married my Demba."

He gazed fondly at his wife for a moment. "But I am not only Diwarna. This I also have to recognize. Ha, enough of such serious thoughts. I am famished. Let us eat something."

There was no order when we sat to dine, unlike in a Mora household. Any took a place where they wished, as do the Diwarna. And 'any' included a number of women and men who served Gordie in one way or another, coming and going. In Mora style, the food was spread on an open porch.

I saw Gordie beckon Pahe and whisper something to him. Soon after, the warrior reappeared with my nets. Gordie's nets now, if he was buying them from me. He spread one out and began to speak of it to those in attendance. Some showed interest, some seemed not to care.

"You will not want to get a crocodile into your net!" said one man.

Oorto added, "Nor one of the great catfish. Some of them are as long as a canoe."

"I am going to give these to some of the tribes," announced Gordie. His eyes momentarily flickered to me and then back to those who had crowded around. "It will not be long before many more will want one. Perhaps our friend Hito can bring them."

Perhaps I could. But more and more I was realizing that being a trader was not for me. I yearned to go searching for stones, not to carry goods from one place to another, trying to convince people to buy.

"We shall keep one for ourselves. It wouldn't hurt to have some fish around here now and again," he finished. Good enough. Just

GOD OF RAIN

remember to pay me.

23. The Shaman

Of course, someone had to teach them how use the nets. Not a man nor woman there had ever thrown a cast-net. That was good for they could not tell that I was no expert either. We practiced the next morning and even pulled a few fish from the river before Gordie's house.

"You will want to go looking for your metals, I think," said Gordie as we shared a lunch. "I need to be off again tomorrow but will leave orders to help you in this."

"I was thinking," I said, "that this would not be a bad place to grow some kalina. You could make your own nets, then. Ropes, too, naturally."

"I fear my people would smoke it all," joked Gordie.

"There is profit in that trade too."

I could see he was thinking about it. "I will not search long, I think," I continued. "Maybe a ten-night visiting the foothills and then head back to my home." Even if I wasn't going to make a life as a trader, I could stick with it for a while, bring more goods up in a month or two. Maybe I should head for the Falls first to obtain more lead. I still intended to increase my wealth. For Mehetu? Maybe. Maybe just to be successful. I didn't know.

"You will need a guide. Not one of my men, I think. They are as likely to get lost as you."

"I could just go up the Gurang. I have done that before and one can't lose his way."

He nodded. "You are as likely to find nuggets there as anywhere."

"And if I do, that would be a start." We both nodded. It seemed a good plan.

Gordie seemed to think for a moment, uncertain whether to speak further. "I understand why you decided to look around here, rather than in your homeland," he said. "Anything you found there would never be yours, really."

This was true. The nobles, the kings, would claim any source I found within their borders. I had not thought this through, perhaps, only telling myself I needed more freedom to search, but some part of me surely knew it.

It was later that Oorto came to me. "I could take you to the Gurang, my friend," he said. "It would be good to travel together again."

"As long as we do not go all the way over the mountains this time."

Oorto answered this seriously. "There is nothing over there for me. But I, ah, do — speak with Hurasu at times." I knew he could communicate with the Lord of Visions from afar. Had I not seen it more than once? "I think he felt the loss of Rahaita almost as much as I."

"But none felt it as did Marareta." There was no question of that.

Oorto sighed deeply. "I walked with Rahaita through the infinite worlds, wandered and gazed upon things you might never imagine, and that too is a great loss. She who became a sister to me is gone. But though we both loved her, in very different ways, Marareta truly loved her as no other."

"You were Marareta's best friend in this world. You still are, I think."

"But we are unlikely to ever again see much of each other. Our lives travel along paths that never meet, only draw close now and then."

"Then is your path leading you where it should, Friend Oorto?"

"I think so. I was meant to be a shaman of my people and so I am. I help them as I can."

"There is more to life than that. This I know, my friend."

"As do I. Have you seen Ulani recently?" I would not have mentioned the storyteller, who had once been his lover.

"He is well. I think he spends all his time thinking of his craft."

"I know how that is. I do the same."

This led me to remember words spoken by A'auwa. "Pana'a believes the son of Marareta will have powers such as hers and Rahaita's. Or yours." Pana'a would not mind me telling Oorto of this; of all men, he would best understand.

Oorto seemed surprised. "I might not have expected this, considering what I was told by Hurasu. Usually, there is the heritage of sorcery — his heritage — in both parents for the gift to manifest. We know Marareta is of another world where there are no wizards."

"Did not Hurasu dwell there for a few centuries?" I asked. "He might have left descendants."

"That is possible. Or even some other sorcerer. The heritage might never show itself there, but sleep within those who carry it."

Almost as an afterthought, he added. "I suspect Malee also shares our gifts."

"They will both need training. Perhaps that is something you are meant to do."

"Perhaps so, my friend, perhaps so."

24. Forest

Layers of leaves, soft and smelling of earth, made no sound, left no mark, as we moved through this forest. The huge smooth trees with their buttressed roots rose like the roof posts of a great house, greater than that of any king, half-light filtering through an endless green vault above.

The buzz of the insects came as if a hundred Kohari musicians were hidden behind the trees, each playing a different tune upon the sef. There were brightly-colored birds flitting barely-seen in the high canopy, flashes of blue and gold and green, and black-and-white monkeys leaping and chattering.

Small patches of forest such as this still stood in the Mora homeland, but nothing so vast. We had walked half a day, Oorto leading me from the more open lands about Gordie's house toward the upper Gurang.

"We shall be there by dark," he assured me, once again. Maybe the Diwarna thought I was nervous here. Perhaps he thought I remembered and feared the leopards and giant monitors that roamed the jungle. I was too in awe for that. This was the greatest of all shrines, a place for gods, not men like we.

Yet Oorto seemed unaffected. Does this world no longer hold wonders when one has walked in others? Or was it simply long familiarity?

"Your people have gods, do they not?" I asked.

"We have very many gods. They are invisible and all around us."

The shaman then smiled. Some might say he smirked. "There are —
things all around us that you can not see, but I do not think they
are gods."

That did not sound so good. "Things?"

"Beings that are not bound to one world but float through them
all. They are harmless." His voice became more thoughtful. "I do
not think they see us either, most of the time, for they are not exactly *here*."

Very well. "So then, have you seen any gods?" I recalled Pana'a
saying that Oorto could probably find one.

"Maybe. It depends on what you think a god is. Hurasu had the
powers of a god, did he not?"

"But he was not a god." I was sure of that.

"What of a sorcerer who had twice his power? Or twice that?
When does one stop being a wizard and become a deity?"

I laughed. "And what of I who had not the slightest portion of
his power? How little must one become to *not* be a god?"

"Little enough to know he is not one, perhaps," came Oorto's
quite sensible reply. "Listen!"

"The wind?" I asked. "No, it is the river, isn't it?" It was no more
than a murmur, distant.

The shaman nodded. "My people consider the Gurang a god,
too. It is certainly powerful."

"I wonder if it knows," was my only possible answer to that.

Oorto ignored my quip. "We are still well below the first falls,
but the banks are solid here. We can walk as far upriver as we
wish."

Soon after, we stood beside the Gurang, still a very broad river at this place and flowing swiftly, foam and debris hurrying past on their way to the sea. "There are crocodiles here, are there not?" I asked. I was admittedly nervous about that.

"There are. The big crocodiles of the saltwater marshes do come up this far sometimes." Although he smiled I knew his warning was serious. "So do not walk too near the water!"

Forest still rose to our right, day disappearing into the shadow of the towering trees. One did not realize quite how high they stood when one was among them. I knew that jungle would thin out as we moved eastward toward the mountains. Just how far that would be, I had no idea. I must trust my guide.

"We have some sunlight left," Oorto said. "Let us move on before we camp."

We trudged along, keeping our cautious distance from the Gurang's flow. There were wide sandy banks here, easy enough to traverse, though soft and wet at places, sucking at our feet and slowing us. I saw only the long-nosed crocodiles, those who ate mostly fish, sunning themselves along our way. Their green-black bodies would slither into the water long before we reached them.

Across the river, the banks rose higher, rockier, and forested hills stood close behind. Did tribes of Diwarna dwell over there, somewhere? I had never heard mention of any.

But I had more pressing questions. "Have you ever seen any of those stones I seek?" I asked Oorto.

"I never looked for them," was his reply. "But my people do pick up such pebbles here, the ones you called sun-stones." He thought a moment before continuing. "Also green stones that seem made of the same substance. We use them to make paint."

I knew of those green stones. It could be good to find some but it was those I named star-stones that I truly hoped to discover. Or even gold or lead. All were useful, though it would be far to carry them.

I would see none here. We needed to be further up the Gurang, where the way grew rocky. Any pebbles would be lost in this sand we crossed.

We camped that night atop a sandy bluff, the forest still behind us. In the dark, I heard the cough of the leopard and many other sounds I did not know, yet I slept well enough.

25. At the Falls

Here and there, now, I would stop and dawdle, examining a bank of small stones washed into some cove. I found nothing and we would move on. I felt very much as if I did not know what I was doing. Ah, but there was only one way to learn.

"We should stop at the falls," decided Oorto, "and make our camp. Then you may search up and down both sides of the river from there." It seemed sensible and as good a plan as any. The water grew increasingly 'angry,' as the Diwarna put it, the Gurang narrowing and rocks sometimes jutting from its surface.

This travel was taking too much time! I would have no more than three days to seek my stones once we stopped. Then we must return — perhaps I should have planned for a longer search. When I returned to these lands, I would do so.

When? If, I should say. There was no reason for me to do this. It was not stones I truly sought; this I knew. A light rain was falling, a rain such as Teva was said to bring. It rained much as we drew closer to the mountains, but never stormed.

I remembered the falls when I had passed this way before. There were several low steps the Gurang tumbled over and down, less than the height of a man put together. Above them the river was still broad, but too wild for a canoe to travel.

Below was a sort of lake, much of it covered with the foam churned up by the plummeting stream. I remembered too the water dragon we had spied there. We glimpsed no others but knew they lived by and in the river.

The roar of that river descending came to us long before we reached the lake. "It is easy enough to cross the Gurang at the falls," Oorto informed me. "That is one reason it is a good place for us to stop." The river beside us narrowed, rushing swiftly, and then widened again as we saw the falls before us.

"Until we went into the mountains I had never traveled further up the river than this spot," my guide told me. "Nor have I since. I do not think I want to place my feet again upon that road."

It was not quite dark so I slowly moved along a bar of small, water-smoothed stones, eyes down, while Oorto went ahead. I was willing to let him choose our campsite. There — ah, no, it was only a shiny crystal of some sort, reddish. Of no value to me but I knew some prized such baubles, so I slipped it into my belt-pouch. I could search in earnest tomorrow.

"There are still crocodiles even here," Oorto reminded me when I reached them. "A man-eater is unlikely this far up, but one never knows. Be watchful!"

"Would not the water dragons chase them away?" I asked, not too seriously. I took a seat on one of the boulders. It had been a weary way and I would seek only rest now.

"They might hunger too, and not hesitate to see how you tasted." I searched his dark face to see if he was jesting. "I have never heard of it happening," the Diwarna continued, "but we both know how their flying relatives are."

We did. Dangerous and capricious those creatures were, and cunning as well. As intelligent as men, some said. More intelligent, others claimed, and definitely just as untrustworthy. "Will we be safe camping near them?" I wondered.

"I've never heard of them bothering a camp. Not when men were there, though they will steal anything left unattended."

I shall admit that I slept with my sword close at hand that night.

Oorto was not in our camp when I awoke. Ah, there by the water, dawn's light shining on his bush of sun-colored hair. He was washing, of course; that was part of his ritual, as much symbolic as anything else. I did note that he bathed near the falling water, where it was shallow and nothing could approach him unseen.

"I shall hunt today," Oorto announced on his return. As always and as most Diwarna, he carried his long spear and thrower. He looked toward the Gurang. "But not fish, I think. I do not know how the dragons might feel about me doing so here."

"We could always ask them," I told him. "I'll go up that way, I think." I pointed east, upriver. "Maybe the other side tomorrow."

All that day I scoured the banks of the Gurang, among great rocks and lesser ones, along banks and bars of pebbles. I found more pretty stones, green and red and some the color of dawnstone. I found chunks of the hard glass that is prized for weapons — that, I could definitely trade for a profit. But none of the metals I sought were to be found.

I gazed across the Gurang that evening, contemplating the northern shore. Tomorrow I would start over there, going upriver, and perhaps further down the flow the next day. Then, I must return to the land of men and leave this one to the unseen dragons in the water and the great condors that flew high above.

26. In the Water

Did I find anything of worth that next day? I found that the Gurang was not so easy to cross as Oorto claimed, as I waded through swiftly flowing shallow water, ever ready to take me off my feet and over one of the falls. Or over all of them. Once I did reach the far side, I again searched the banks for my stones.

I found more of what I had before. I found, too, one lone pebble of dawn-stone, gold. That, I considered promising for if one metal was here then why not others? Yes, yes, I know there is no logic to that; it is like saying if pelicans are on the beach, why not parrots?

I laid out these treasures in the evening and examined them. They and those gathered before would hardly begin to fill up my large pack-basket, which I had insisted on bringing. Better to have space left over than not enough space. There was still a day left.

"No sun-stone," observed Oorto, looking over my shoulder. "I speared a marmot. Come and eat." That was fare I had not tasted since we shared it in the mountains. Nor had Oorto, I suspected. The creatures did not live near his home in the swamps.

"I did watch for your stones while I hunted," he said, as we settled down beside the fire. "I do not think they grow here but only wash down from the mountains."

"Probably so, my friend," I agreed. "On the other hand, there could great chunks of sun-stone beneath our feet."

Oorto laughed. "Where should we begin to dig?"

"Had I any sense," I replied, "I would be home digging a garden."

That sounded good to me, I realized, though I had spoken in jest. I would rather do that than wander through these rocks. But there was no sense in thinking of that. "I shall go downstream on the far side tomorrow. Whether I find anything or not, that will be enough time spent here."

I took a bite of the meat. "As gamy as I remembered," I told Oorto.

That night, I awoke and saw Oorto sitting upright, unmoving, in the dark. I thought I knew what he was doing and felt it best to say nothing. After a time, he seemed to relax and lay down to sleep. I, too, returned to slumber.

Through our breakfast, I said nothing of this to the subdued shaman. At last, I spoke. "You visited those other worlds last night."

"I spoke with Hurasu. He sensed that I was approaching the borders of his realm, that I was near the start of his ancient road, and wondered of this."

"What did you tell him?"

"The truth. He seemed amused." Oorto, for a moment, seemed far away. "And maybe also troubled that the Mora seek such things. I can tell you that he was not surprised you were the one doing this." I had thought Hurasu barely noted my existence. That he remembered anything about me came as a surprise.

It mattered not. I would never see the man again, I was certain. "If I find nothing today he will have no reason to be troubled," I stated. "I might as well get as much in as I can." I rose and prepared to cross the river. The Gurang was cold here, at least compared to that part of it that flowed through the jungles and swamps further west. I knew it grew far icier in the mountains.

The Gurang's banks rose higher and rockier on the north side. This I had noted previously. They became even more so as I moved downstream this morning. There were fewer bars and coves that I might search and, for a time, they yielded nothing. Then, I found my first nugget of sun-stone.

I was sure of it this time. The bright metal showed here and there through a green patina. It was not large, no bigger than a ground nut, but it was something, at last. There was copper some where along this river or those streams that flowed into it.

I made my way further along the riverbank, though it became ever more difficult. At places, there were only a few rocks to scramble across at the base of the low cliffs. Then I reached a rocky outcrop, overhanging the river. My way was blocked. Could I make my way to the top and continue there?

Or this might be the time to turn around, a sign that my search was done. What was that? Something glittered there, in the face of the rocky bank, just beyond my reach. I was sure it was sun-stone. If only I could edge out and see. Yes, hold onto that rock that protruded there.

Then I was in the water, as was the rock I had grasped, broken from the cliff-face. The current grabbed me with its cold hands, threw me against the rock wall, and for a moment I knew nothing.

27. Swept Away

It was my good luck that it was only for a moment or I would have never left the Gurang that day. For a moment more, I was dazed and unable to think clearly, though I was aware enough to keep myself afloat. I was being swept past the high banks and could see no place to take hold and climb.

The other side? It was far but I was a strong swimmer. No, surely there would be a spot where I could get out of the water and I did not wish to risk encountering a crocodile out there. I let myself be carried along.

There! No, in an instant I was torn from my handhold. From where I bobbed in the water, it appeared ever higher cliffs rose further down the Gurang and, worse, hung out over the flow. I must make for the opposite shore.

Now must I do it, before I floated down to where it grew swampy and there was no shore to find over there. I began to stroke toward my distant goal, still being carried swiftly downriver.

Something surfaced, a long dark body breaking the water and then disappearing again. I had no time to assess its size nor even to be sure whether it was one of the great saltwater crocodiles or one of the lesser breeds. Those, too, would attack a creature that struggled in the water. So it would end for Hito, far from his home, never finding those things he sought.

My prayer went up to the first god who came to mind and that was Teva. Yes, that surprised me too, but who better than a god of peace when one prepares to depart the world?

Two other forms, sleek, brown, surfaced near me and then dove. Though I barely glimpsed them, I knew them to be water dragons. Were they challenging the crocodile, hoping to make me their meal rather than his?

Their was little evidence of whatever turmoil took place under the water. Once the crocodile's tail appeared, lashing back and forth, before it was again hidden by the Gurang. A swirl here, a bit of foam there. If these dragons used tactics anything like those that flew, they would be using their agility to nip at their adversary and then dart away again. I did not think they could kill a big crocodile, even a pair of them, but they could certainly discourage it.

It was not long before two rounded, fur-covered heads popped out of the water. They chirped at each other and maybe at me. Might it be that they did not intend to make a meal of me? All the while, we floated further down the river.

And I had been pushed back toward the shore I had tried to swim away from. I spied a snag, a branch or small tree protruding close to the rocky banks and managed to reach and hang on to it. I turned and saw no sign of my two rescuers, only the broad Gurang. They might be lurking no more than a few feet beneath me, I knew.

I could feel that my sword still hung at my side, and my bag was yet on my belt. To jettison one or both would have been wise but I could not bring myself to do this. I turned back to the rocks that hung out over the water above me. There was no getting up here.

But there, not too much far further down, I could see water

gushing, where some little stream added its flow to that of the Gu-rang. Perhaps there would be enough of a break in the cliff to get up. I somewhat reluctantly released my hold and let myself be carried down, attempting to slow my movement by grasping at the wall beside me. It tore my hands but I could not risk being swept past my goal.

Yes, yes, the cliffs were broken here and there was enough of a recess that I could pull myself out of the current. The water of the stream poured upon me but that I did not mind. I could make my way up, I thought, up and over the slippery boulders. There would be a reach, there at the top — best not concern myself with that until I was at it.

Slowly, carefully, I crept upward, forcing myself not to rush, to be patient. Not so long did I climb, I am sure, but it was as much a journey, in its way, as the crossing of the mountains. I placed hands and feet in cracks, on the slightest bump or depression, all the while drenched by the tumbling water. Then, I had no choice but to balance, reaching, risking at the last. I grasped the lip of the cliff and pulled myself to the top. Less than the height of two men was I above the river, and forest rose before me. I turned and sat, weary, there on the edge of that cliff, gazing out over the Gurang. Two sleek heads rose from the water, glittering black eyes regarded me. I waved and they sank into the river, not to reappear.

I knew not how to thank a water dragon. I knew not why they had aided me. Maybe they just disliked crocodiles. But I did thank them, and the gods, as well.

So where was I?

28. Alone

I was certainly not going to attempt to cross the wide Gurang again. That was a lesson learned! The falls must be far above me but my best choice was to begin walking back to them. Oorto might or might not still be waiting by the time I returned. Be that as it may, I could cross the river there and seek a way to return to the house of Gordie.

If I did not starve first! I had no weapons other than sword and knife, neither suitable for hunting. There was nothing to do but begin trudging along the top of these high banks. First, though, I looked down into the shallow pool carved into the rock by this little stream, just above where it fell to the Gurang, and saw several pebbles of copper.

There was no reason not to scoop them up and add them to the one in my pouch. Somewhere up there, I thought, turning my eyes toward the north, there is more of this sun-stone. Not today could I seek it; I turned my feet to begin my journey.

Four days I traveled, scrambling up and down gullies, turning aside where I must, fearing to stray too far from the river's bank and become lost in the forest. My hunger gnawed at me, for I had gone long without food. But the falls lay before me at last.

Oorto had gone. This did not surprise me; surely he thought me dead. The Diwarna would have waited two days, or three, and had no doubt searched for me, but eventually he would have returned to the house of Gordie with his bad news. There was nothing to be done about that. First I should try to feed myself.

Would that I had brought one of my cast-nets with me! But a sharpened stick, a spear, would be enough, and I made one at once. Oorto might have hesitated to take fish here but I was too hungry to care. In the shallow pools between the falls, I was able to pierce a small whitish bottom-feeder nosing about the rocks. Almost did I devour it raw, right there as I stood to my knees in the Gurang's flow.

Instead I ate it raw on the river bank. It was bony. Two more I caught and consumed before I began to feel not so hollow. I would rest there tonight, I decided, and try to spear some more fish before I left. There might be another long hungry trek ahead of me.

The forest route by which Oorto had led me here was out of the question. I would soon have been lost among those trees. No, I would need to stay further east, on the higher, more open ground, and try to find my way around to a familiar country. Maybe I could retrace the way I had come from the trade village with Marareta two years before. Before striking out and searching in that direction, though, I should travel down the Gurang a short way.

I slept deeply that night and started out the next morning, taking the time to spear several more fish first. Some I consumed there, immediately; some I would take with me, after gutting them and packing them with wet grass. It was always possible that Gordie would send men this way to look for me so I might not want to leave the river bank too soon. There was no advantage to hurrying now. I had no place to hurry to.

I took the time to make fire that evening, roasting my remaining fish. It was definitely better so. Sometime tomorrow I should leave the river, I told myself as I fell into exhausted slumber. Sometime tomorrow.

When I awoke, a number of men were seated on the ground about me. Kohari. Four, I could see when I sat up and sleep left my eyes. One of them had my pouch. He pulled out a nugget and looked at it. "Sometimes we seek these here too, man of the Mora." He put the pebble back, pulling the tie-strings tight and replacing the bag among my things. Then they were traders. That seemed sensible. Who else would come so far up the Gurang?

"You are lost?" asked another.

"Some might say so," I replied, to laughter all around.

One looked more closely at me. "You are Hito, no? I saw you at the Great Falls." He turned to his fellows. "He was companion to the Hero from the Sea." There was murmuring and knowing nods of the head.

"Then he is fortunate he met us and not one of the war bands," spoke the first man again, whom I took to be their leader. "Maybe we can help you find your way home, Hito of the Mora."

"That would be most appreciated," I answered, "but I think you know the way no better than I." That, too, brought laughs. Then I had to tell the tale of how I came to be where I was. It needed no embellishment! We ate of the food they carried with them, dried fish and the kuru fruit. Even these tasted good to me then.

"We might find a Diwarna to carry you where you need to be," said their captain. "But they are wary of us."

"I don't blame them," spoke another, and spat. As many Kohari traders, they had a low opinion of the warriors who raided for no reason other than to take captives or heads. If nothing else, it hurt their profits.

"Or we can take you all the way to the Great Falls," said the leader. "We will not charge you too much! Come, board our boat and we shall see what is to be done."

29. Taken

I knew the river on which Gordie had his compound would be difficult to find. It joined the Gurang in a swampy morass, with no clear channel to follow. I knew too that Gordie preferred it be difficult to find.

"We came upriver to trade with the Diwarna," I was told. "We usually would not have gone as far as where we found you."

Another said, "The hope was to hunt for some fresh meat. We were growing tired of fish and kuru."

"I was tired of kuru long ago," I responded. "I grew up eating far too much of it." The bland fruit was a staple in some areas, for those of little wealth. It did not thrive in the cooler lands of the east, where they rose toward the mountains, and was not seen so much there.

"It is said your people brought the kuru to these coasts," said Wolak, the leader of this group. "We do eat a great deal of the fruit, and use its bark to make cloth." He slapped at the side of his vessel. "Much of this boat is built of its wood."

Their boat was the typical basket-shaped Kohari craft, made of pieces of wood sewn together with fiber and caulked with some sort of resin. It would be good to know what that was, would it not? There was a mast but the square mat sail was not raised right now, nor was much rowing necessary as we floated on the Gurang's current. It was small, and packed with trade goods, primarily crocodile hides and the craft-work of the Diwarna.

"We are done trading here so we do not mind giving you a ride. But we were headed back to our own lands and you would not wish to go there." Mora traders did sail to the Kohari coasts sometimes, but it was dangerous. The folk there were too unpredictable, welcoming visitors one day, trying to take their heads the next. It had not always been so, the old stories said.

"I say we sail south," chimed in one of the men. "We can do business at the Falls as well as anywhere else."

"You don't have a wife waiting for you," replied another.

The captain said, "I do have a wife but I see that as a good argument not to sail home right away. I say the Falls." There was only one dissenter and he did not seem that adamant about it. Maybe his wife was prettier than Wolak's.

"But if we do make contact with the Diwarna, we'll hand you over to them," decided Wolak. "We usually just tie up at certain places along the river and someone eventually shows up."

"We don't want to spend more time here, now that we have finished trading," added one of the others.

Wolak nodded. "There's a spot up ahead where we can sit for a little while. If no one shows, we'll head for Gurang-mouth."

It looked much like any other spot on the river but I took their word for it. This was swamp land here, interspersed with patches of higher jungle. In the height of the rainy season, water flowed through both. I think I dozed off.

"Down," came an order. Someone pushing me. "Cover him." They were arranging their trade goods to conceal me. What was going on?

"We seek offerings for the goddess," came a thick, low-pitched voice.

Wolak responded. "Those with whom we trade are not be attacked. That is custom."

"Not my custom. We could take your heads too," came the arrogant reply.

"We are also protected!" objected Wolak. "Traders are not to be taken. The priests have decreed it." The man remained calmer than I might have.

"One head looks like another when severed from its body." I heard what I assumed to be men climbing into our boat. A moment later I was uncovered.

"A Mora!" exclaimed one of the men. There was no hiding that fact. Perhaps, with time to prepare, I could pass for a man of the Kohari — we do not look so different. But everything about me, my clothing, my hair, my tattoos, proclaimed who I was.

I was pulled to my feet. Two Kohari boats, each of them half again as long as the one in which I rode, and a dozen warriors could I see. My new friends could not stand against these men, nor should they.

"We have found another prize to carry back with us. Bring him!" ordered the chieftain.

Wolak looked as though he wanted to say something, but held his tongue. He needed to think of his own men now, not me.

"A Mora trader?" asked that deep, growling voice.

"Yes, mighty Bohasuk," spoke one of the traders. "We were returning him to the Diwarna." The man who said this looked upon me impassively, giving no indication that he knew anything more of me. I would have done the same.

"Ha. You should not have hidden him from me." Bohasuk fixed his heavy-lidded eyes on each trader in turn. "I should slay you all but you are not worth it."

I was thrust into one of the boats, beside two other bound prisoners, both Kohari. Of a different tribe, I suspected; the Kohari are ever warring among themselves. More disturbing, I could see severed heads in a basket nearer the prow.

"We shall take this Mora we captured back to the temple," announced Bohasuk to his warriors. Captured? Stumbled over, more like it. "We have done well on our voyage. It is time to return."

I turned to my comrades-in-bonds. "Bohasuk is a great coward," whispered one. "Those were only fisherman, minding their own business when he swooped down on them." He nodded toward the basket. "Killed them all, even the women."

"The children too," mumbled the other. "And they used the women before slaying them." Undisguised hatred was in the eyes he turned on our captors. "We shall be following them. We all shall die on the altar of the Sun Bird."

30. A Captive

My bronze sword remained on the boat of the Kohari traders. Better there than in the hands of these men, I felt. Would they get word to anyone or simply forget about me and go about their business?

"But you are not fishermen, are you?" I asked the man who had first spoken to me.

The Kohari answered with pride. "We are warriors of our tribe, captured fairly and in battle. We do not wish to die in the temple but we would have done the same to Bohasuk if able. I accept my fate."

"Fool," snarled his companion. "I accept nothing. We kill and kill for no reason." He scowled at the bottom of the boat for a moment before going on. "Bohasuk slew those fishermen because taking them was a dishonorable deed. As he said, one head looks like another. He cares not for honoring Mihasa but only for increasing his own reputation."

The two boats raced down the Gurang, sails and oars adding to the push of the current. These Kohari were in a hurry to get home, perhaps to bask in a reputation as successful raiders. They were young men, almost all, some no more than boys.

I was not mistreated, nor were my fellow prisoners. Once we reached the open sea, our bonds were removed. Where could we go? No Kohari would willingly leap into the sea to kill himself, for they saw it as the abode of demons, a place where the evil went after death, home to the great snake Bagap. I feared not the sea but was not ready for suicide.

"We must be kept healthy for the sacrifice," confided one of my fellow prisoners — we never exchanged names so I can not give you one for him. "It would be dishonorable to give Mihasa those who are sick or starved."

I have never been a sailor, never taken canoe into the deep sea nor further north than the point of Ahurataca, which marks the end of the Mora realm. I know only that we sailed north, remaining close to the coast, for Kohari are timid sailors. That coast stood steep and rock-bound, mountains rising from the sea, once we were past the mangrove marshes of the Gurang basin. The high waves crashed upon the uninhabited shore, white plumes rising and falling among the sea-worn rocks.

And we were fed kuru. That I consider a form of torture. Ah, not truly. Who could hate the bland taste of the kuru fruit? It only brought memories to me of childhood, life without a father, depending on the charity of relatives. I chose the way of a warrior early and left that behind.

I know we rounded a headland at last, the end of a long peninsula, and entered a gulf of sorts, the heart of the Kohari nation. I saw many of their boats here, and villages along the shores. The Kohari were a numerous people. Across that gulf lay the great isle on which many also resided and on which their temple of Mihasa, the Sun Bird, stood.

The many tribes of the Kohari brought prisoners there to be sacrificed, vying each to provide greater numbers than the other.

Thus, they raided each other, warring constantly, and none growing too strong. This the priests approved for it gave them more power.

The temple itself was a place of truce, where any could come and go in peace. Bohasuk and another chief might come at the same time, each with prisoners captured from the other, and could not attack each other, nor even complain. It was how things were — a man captured and brought to the temple belonged now to Mihasa and no chieftain could claim him.

An army of Mora had burnt that temple to the ground not so long ago, Poneiva and Marareta among them. What stood now at that spot?

Soon, I would know.

Part III. The Kohari

31. The Temple

There was a stockade, thick tree trunks sunk into the ground, and a wide and heavy timber double-gate. This was as the temple had been described to me by those who had raided it. I knew not whether this was a new palisade or if that one had escaped the flames.

I had not been with the party that attacked the Kohari here more than three years before, freeing the captives and burning the temple. Those captives were the companions of Marareta, those who had come from the sea with him. Amirea, wife of Aranu, was among them, as was her father Neatanu and the hero Bafa. How different might things have been had they died on the altar of Mihasa?

That the temple itself was still being rebuilt I could see as we entered those gates. The partially finished structure was surrounded by many smaller buildings, low huts mostly. The temple would rise high above them when it was completed, higher than even the house of the High King, but built in the same manner, post and beam. I, who had seen the fortresses of Hurasu, was not impressed.

Before the temple stood the altar, on an elevated platform supported by carved timbers. There was the snake Bagap, his form wrapped about the bottom, and the burnished representation of Mihasa, the Sun Bird, above, of hammered sun-stone. It must be new — surely that would have melted when the temple burned.

Bohasuk led us in, holding a heavy spear and strutting in triumph. His young followers emulated him, mistaking his pose for that of a warrior. Had any ever been in true battle? He was a large man, by Kohari standards, standing a little taller than me. Many Mora would have towered above him.

The severed heads Bohasuk had distributed to his men, so they might offer them individually and gain honor. So does a leader win loyalty. But what honor was there in those heads? They would gain no mana from them, if that was what they sought, only empty words of praise.

A knot of priests came out to look us over. There were suspicious glances at the heads the boys carried, but nothing was said of them. All wore wide, ornate collars, and high headdresses, not unlike the crowns of Mora priests and nobles, but made of bark-cloth, not feathers.

He with the highest crown was undoubtedly the High Priest. First he looked to my two fellow-prisoners. "Take them," the priest told his attendants. He then looked me over. "The Mora we shall save for the festival." I assume my two companions died within the next few days, for I never saw them again after they were led away.

"Saruk," he continued, addressing one of the lesser priests, "take these young warriors to the altar so they may present their gifts." There might have been the slightest sarcasm in the man's voice, but one does not become High Priest without also being a skilled politician. That is true anywhere.

Bohasuk's men filed away, eagerly following their guide. The priest's eyes returned to me. "Show our guest to his quarters!" he ordered, laughing. "Come, Lord Bohasuk, and have palm wine with me."

Where the two went to drink, I know not, for two temple guards took charge of me, led by one of the priests. As all Kohari — male or female — they dressed in long kilts of bark-cloth, printed with designs that made no sense to me. The tattoos of a Mora body, the signs painted upon a Mora canoe, these I could read.

Bits of copper jewelry shown on the priest's wrists, but the warriors wore no ornaments. They did carry stout, flint-tipped spears.

Into a windowless hut I was thrust, one with walls of wood not unlike the hulls of their boats. There would be no breaking through them. "Take his clothes," ordered the priest. It was but a simple loincloth but they must have it, and left me naked in the dark.

Not completely dark, I realized, as my eyes grew accustomed to my surroundings. The door, a heavy wooden affair, contained a small window allowing a meager light into the place. I had seen no doors in several seasons, for the Mora do not use them. I went to it and peered out. No one was to be seen but only a few feet away stood a wall of the temple itself.

A crude clay pot was placed in one corner. I could surmise its purpose. Bedding, a straw of some sort. It smelled fresh. The Kohari took care of their sacrifices, I knew this. They would feed me, possibly allow me to bathe. But it was unlikely I would leave this hut, this house of sacrifices, until I was led before the altar of Mihasa.

There was nothing more to be done, so I lay down and slept.

32. Recognized

It was the guards who brought me an evening meal. Kuru, again, but baked well and with some seasoning I did not know. Kohari food tends to be more highly flavored than that to which I was accustomed. The men did not seem to mind conversing with me, seemed friendly, even. "Why did you take my loincloth?" I asked.

A laugh. "You must be presented naked to the goddess," was the answer. They could have waited. "You will not need it again, Mora." The two spoke the pidgin as well as any traders might. Here, where Kohari of many tribes came together, that would be necessary.

And so I waited. I slept, I ate. I watched those who served at the temple pass by my little window, both women and men, some of the priesthood, some those who served them. It was a much-used corridor, it seemed.

How long it would be until the festival in which I was to be slain, I had no idea. It would have something to do with the position of the sun, surely. All Kohari holy days mark such things. Could I escape? Unlike the fatalistic Kohari prisoners, ready to go to their deaths, I was determined to seek a way out. If nothing else, it gave me something to do.

Yes, if only I might slip out of here somehow, steal a boat. Was I wrong to hope for such a thing? I yearned only to return to the land of the Mora, to find rest beside A'auwa, and forget those things that brought me here. And who would rest beside me? That

I could not see.

It was on my third day there that Bohasuk himself came to see me. He spoke only through the door, putting his ugly face to the window. With great effort, I kept myself from punching it. "We have learned who you are, Mora," he announced. "It is told up and down the coasts that the mighty warrior Hito disappeared on the Gurang."

There was no point in denying this. "It is so," I admitted.

"The friend of the Hero from the Sea and of those who burnt the temple. Many will wish to come and see your end, dog." His laugh was scornful. "I shall make sure to be here."

And to make sure, as well, that everyone knew he was responsible for my taking. How might a man become so vain?

"We hope your friends return and attempt to rescue you. We will be ready this time!" he taunted, and left me.

The Kohari hoped to set a trap, with Hito as bait? I knew well that there were those who might try to rescue me. All the more reason to get away and warn them not to come — not that my scheduled sacrifice were not cause enough.

Gossip spreads quickly in a compound such as this temple. Soon, my identity was know to all and I became a curiosity. Many came to look at me, and asked me for my tales. I saw no reason not to speak to them, though escape remained foremost in my mind.

Could I pick out the resin between the boards, force my way through a wall? That approach seemed unlikely to succeed, nor had I any tools with which to attempt it. Perhaps through the thatched roof — if only I could reach it. Time and again, I tried to scale the walls, bracing myself in a corner, without reaching even half the distance.

I did this at night when none would see, and I would continue to try. What else could I do?

Another morning came, another day of captivity. There came also giggles outside my door, and one face after another took its turn peeking in. Normally, I might not mind having no loincloth but I was not sure I liked being so on display! I went to the door to see who was there. It was both amusing and slightly disconcerting that the girl currently at the window craned her head to see my lower regions.

"My greetings, women of the temple," I said. There were several of them out there, mostly young, mostly rather small and slender. Some would have needed to stand on tiptoe to peek in.

A chorus of greetings was returned to me, and more giggling.

"You are priestesses?" I asked.

That brought true laughter. "No, we are dancers, foolish Mora," one told me. They seemed to find it humorous that I could not tell the difference.

"Ah. It is too bad I can not watch you dance, little ones."

Another spoke up. "You will behold us dancing before the altar of Mihasa before you —" She seemed to think better of continuing that thought.

"Don't say that," scolded one of her companions.

"It is a great waste," one girl stated, rather glumly. For the most part, the other dancers nodded their heads in agreement.

A priestess — yes, the difference was obvious, wasn't it? — came along and clucked at them. "You should be in the temple. Move along."

"But come back later!" I called after them. I was sure they would provide better company than my guards who brought the inevitable kuru.

33. Visitors

"Yes, my Lord Hidlat, this should be it." A dark face peered in at me. I could see by his headdress that the man was a priest. Over to the door I went, so I might see the rest of him.

Two visitors stood outside my prison, the priest and a man I took for a noble. "I thank you, Brother Dywa," said the nobleman. "Do you wish to remain?"

"I would be honored, my lord," replied the priest. He was not a young man. A tuft of white hair stood from his chin, adding character to a round, bland face. The noble turned back to my window.

"I am Hidlat," he said. "I greet you, Hito."

"My greetings, Lord Hidlat." Now this fellow looked like a true warrior, though he was a bit squat. A scar ran directly across his face, leaving a deep mark in his flat nose. But appearances are but appearances.

"I have heard of you," Hidlat stated. "I regret that you must end here."

"Perhaps there is something you could do about that, my lord?" It hurt not to suggest it.

He shook his head. "It is done. You belong to Mihasa." Hidlat cocked his head at me. "How could one such as Bohasuk have bested you?"

I gave him the story of that. At many points, he nodded knowingly. "It might be argued that you should not have been taken," he said at its ending, "as a trader. Or, at least, being in the protection of traders."

"I would not doubt that this Bohasuk would have simply taken all our heads if Wolak had objected."

"This is so. Their lives were saved, though yours is forfeit."

"We could complain formally," spoke the priest.

"No," replied Lord Hidlat. "The High Priest desires this man's life. He would hear no objections."

"He remembers the attack here."

"Many do." The noble turned back to me. "Can anything be done to make your days easier?" he asked. "It is not good to sit and let your fate weigh upon you."

"You could ask the dancing girls to pass by more frequently," I suggested. "Or even the priestesses, though some of them give me the sourest of looks."

"That," remarked the priest, "may be because they see something they may not have."

Hidlat laughed at that. "It is too bad we can not allow any of the women into your cell. Even the ones with sour faces."

"Well," I said, "if women are out of the question, perhaps I might be fed something other than kuru now and again."

"I shall see about that, Warrior Hito," promised Dywa.

"Ah, but kuru is solid food," spoke Hidlat. "I have marched far on a stomach full of it."

"The tree is a gift from the gods," came Dywa's pious remark.

"A gift from the Mora," Hidlat corrected him. "But it is most useful. Why, our very clothing is made of it."

We Mora did make cloth of the kuru bark but more commonly

used that of the sapa tree, which thrives better in the uplands. The sapa's roots, too, could serve as rope and was used much before kalina was widely grown. "I have heard the Mora brought many things to you," I said. Though perhaps these Kohari would not like to admit to it.

Lord Hidlat answered in the most sober of tones. "Some of your people came to us many generations ago, it is told, and made themselves lords among the Kohari. It was they who taught us that mana may be won through warfare and sacrifice. We have forgotten the gods they brought with them but this we remembered."

"You number them among your own ancestors, my lord," came Dywa's soft voice.

"That I do."

There was a long pause. "That seems not a good thing to bring you," I said. "Those Mora were driven from our land for following such beliefs."

Dywa spoke. "It fitted well with the teachings of our ancient ancestors. The First of our legends, whose substance fills all things and is all things, seemed much like the mana of which they told us."

"And we were already a warlike people," added Hidlat. He sighed. "Would that were not so. I would readily live in peace." His voice sharpened its edge. "But first I would wish to lay the head of Bohasuk before the Sun Bird."

I could see the priest agreed completely with this thought.

"I give you my farewell, Hero of the Mora. I will not like to see you lose your head, but I must attend the ceremony."

"It will not hurt," Dywa whispered to me. "We give you a drug first to numb all the senses."

"It might be argued," said Lord Hidlat, "whether that is for the sake of those sacrificed or so they don't squirm and spoil the ritual."

"It does not matter, my lord, does it?" asked Dywa, as the pair slowly walked away and around the corner.

34. The Dancing Girl

I was again attempting to scale a corner — without success — when I noticed a faint light flicker at my door. None had before visited at night.

It was one of the dancers. I could smell the palm oil burning in the small lamp she carried. "Whatever were you doing, man of the Mora?"

"Exercising," I answered. "I should not be weak when I go to Mihasa." She looked skeptical. "I thank you for coming, woman of the temple." As long as she was being formal, so would I. "It is lonely here, especially at night."

"I wanted you to myself!" she whispered, but rather loudly. "Without all those silly girls crowding around." She giggled. "Yes, Lord Hito, I am one of those silly girls too."

"Not lord," I told her. "I am but a warrior." Or was a warrior. I did not think I wanted to tell this young lady I was a trader now. Her people did not value such men.

She spoke the trade pidgin well enough, and what I took for her native dialect of Kohari was similar, so we could converse without stumbling over too many strange words. "You are named Ranadi?" I asked her. Someone had addressed her so; that I remembered.

She laughed at the question. "That is what we women of the temple call each other. It means — well, it means *ranadi*." This I later found to be a Kohari word for 'sister.'

"My name," she went on, "is Miyawanagayun."

"That is too big a name for such a little one!" I objected. "I shall call you Tamba." That means "companion" in the pidgin and she understood the word.

"I shall be your companion while I may, man of the Mora." Her face of a sudden grew sad, her eyes looked away from me and to the ground. Perhaps she thought of my impending sacrifice. Then, brightening, she added, "But I like my name."

"Then so do I," said I. "But I shall call you Tamba, none the less." My eyes lingered on her for a moment, for she was an attractive girl, but then fixed themselves on the necklace she wore. It was of the star-stones I had sought.

"Why do you stare at my breasts, Mora?" she demanded.

"They are very lovely, Tamba. How can you blame me for being a man?" They were lovely, admittedly, but I was lying. It did not hurt to flatter the girl. "Those stones are sacred to Lugan, are they not?"

She nodded. "Lugan is the patron of we who dance in the temple."

It would do no good to ask her where they came from. She was unlikely to know and it would serve no purpose. Instead, I studied the woman before me. Tamba was pale, was she not? I could see that even by the flickering flame of her oil lamp. Perhaps she never went out into the sun.

"Could you dance for me?" I asked. "I would like to see it before, well, you know."

There, in the little passageway between my hut and the temple, by the light of the lamp she placed on the ground, she went through the intricate moves of her dance. So unlike the Mora dances was it, all angular movements rather than the way our women — and men — swayed. Even our war dances were so.

Tamba was compact, slender, but had a dancer's muscles, smooth and strong beneath her golden skin. Her firm breasts were indeed good to look upon. I had not lied about that.

And around her neck glittered those crystals.

"I must go now, Hito," she told me when she finished. "May I visit again?"

"Anytime," I replied, and then let out a rueful laugh. "Until I am no longer here." Then she was gone, away into the dark.

I had, for a moment, felt sorry for myself and my fate. I did not do such things. To my corner I returned and tried once again to climb to the ceiling.

35. At Night

Others still visited, though my novelty was wearing off. How long it was until my day of sacrifice I did not know, nor did I wish to know. I would only brood if told how many days remained.

And Tamba came often, almost every night, and sometimes one of her friends. We spoke of nothing of import; mostly I spoke, I am afraid, and she listened to my tales. Tamba knew little of the outside world and Mora warriors inhabited the same realm as the demons of her people's legends.

I had given up trying to reach the ceiling. Even when I finally managed to climb the wall, there were no beams to grasp, only boards held together with coconut fiber. I fell too far when I tried to hold onto them.

This does not mean I had given up on attempting to escape. My head would be rolling before Mihasa's image before that happened.

She seemed troubled that night. Before, had I seen her so, but it never lasted once we began to talk. Tonight, it seemed I could not make her forget what bothered her. "What is wrong, little Tamba?" I asked.

I did not think she would tell me, at first, but then it burst out. "It is the priest Punpasay. He is forever after me to lie with him."

"You do not want to be with Punpasay?" I did not know which of the many priests who passed by my cell he might be but I knew I disliked him.

"I am *calansa*," she informed me, with what seemed a touch of pride. I did not know the word and so told her. Tamba's reluctance to explain was obvious but at last she said, "I have never been — um, never had —" She looked directly at me, hoping I would catch the meaning. I did.

"You have had no lovers," I said.

"Mmm, yes. Well, no. No men." She giggled. "We women of the temple are not expected to never enjoy ourselves."

"Ah. Of course not." I didn't understand why anyone would wish to be calansa but they might as well make the best of the situation. The ways of the Kohari are strange. "And what," I asked her, "would happen if you gave in to this priest?"

She shuddered. "If any found out, my head would join those in the temple. But Punpasay," Tamba practically spat out the name, "would only be reprimanded. It is the way here."

"If I could get out of here, I would add Punpasay's head to that pile," I growled.

The dancer gave me a long look but said nothing.

I knew I must not make the mistake of thinking of her as a child, even if she looked like one. Tamba was a woman, a highly disciplined woman. That went with being a dancer, moreover one skilled enough to serve at the central temple of all the Kohari. This she had been trained in since a little girl.

But little else did she know. Her knowledge of the world was slight, her sense of ethics practically nonexistent. She could be quite bloodthirsty when she spoke of the little vendettas and intrigues of the temple, among the dancers themselves, though she seemed demure, submissive even, much of the time.

Naturally, she thought the beheading that occurred here to be part of the ordinary course of things. "You Mora do not take the heads of your enemies?" she asked, astonished on hearing this.

"No, Tamba, we treat the brave dead with honor. They are no longer our enemies when they go to the gods."

"But the dead can come as ghosts and harm us! It is better if they have no heads and can not see us." I could not argue with that, not without plunging into far deeper waters than I wished. And Tamba might drown there.

"So let us deal with the living," I said. "You will not always dance in the temple, will you? Will you someday leave and take a husband?"

She only shrugged. "It may be. Some dancers remain and train those who come to join us. The best dancers — like me!" Tamba giggled over that. "Some do join the priestesses."

"Are they also calansa?" I asked.

She shook her head. "No, they do not have to be. But some do not want men." The girl frowned. "For a time that may be alright but not for a lifetime. None marry, but only take lovers." That was true of some priestesses in my home too. Pana'a came to mind.

"What of the priests?"

"Some take wives. Some marry dancers. That would not be so bad."

"Ah, you have someone in mind?"

"Anyone but Punpasay!" She stood in thought a moment, shifting her lamp from one hand to the other. "It is more likely that I would be taken as wife by some noble who visits the temple. We usually end up as second or third wives for some old man."

"What if you do not wish it?"

She turned her face up to me. "It does not matter. The High Priest gives us to whom he will."

36. Punpasay

"Punpasay says he will accuse me of seducing him if I do not give myself to him," Tamba told me, two nights later. "He threatens to denounce me to the High Priest."

If the girl were truly, as she put it, calansa, then it could easily be proven that his accusations were false. Surely she knew this? I did not bring this up, asking rather, "What will you do?"

"I will let you out of this house and you will take me away," she evenly stated. "I have thought of this for many days."

"The guards?" I knew they were nearby.

"I gave them the drug we give the prisoners," Tamba told me. "The ones to be sacrificed. They sleep." I could see her sly smile by the light of the lamp she held. "It is easy to get hold of the drug. Some of the priests, ah, crave it and must have it often."

I realized suddenly she meant to escape right then. A warning would have been welcome, not that I was ungrateful. The woman was already undoing the catch on the door.

A moment later, I stood outside. "You are tall," she said, looking me up and down.

"And you are small," I replied. Smaller than I had realized, peeking at her through my little window. My people tend to be large, it is true. We are taller, on whole, than the Kohari and heavier, both men and women. As Mora go, I was of an ordinary height but this girl came only to my chest.

I began to wrap the kilt she brought around me. "Best latch the door again," I suggested. "If it is hanging loose, someone might notice it."

Tamba whispered, "I fear Punpasay may be seeking me."

"No need to fear him now." I hoped so, anyway.

"You will kill him for me," she declared.

"Only if he gets in our way, Tamba. We don't want to rouse all the temple." I don't think she liked that but saw the wisdom in it.

Next, I donned a collar. All the Kohari wore collars when dressing for ceremonies, made of bark-cloth, sometimes with strings of shells or beads. The priests wore them always, and those were larger, almost capes, and the High Priest's the largest of all. There were signs painted on mine but I knew not their significance, whether they spoke of status or were symbols of Kohari gods.

Finally, a crown of bark-cloth. That would hide my hair, which was not cut at all in Kohari fashion — their men looked like someone had placed a black bowl atop their heads. I should pass as Kohari well enough at night. I was thankful I did not have the plentiful tattoos of a nobleman!

One more thing was needed. "Did you bring me a weapon?" I asked Tamba

"Oh, I did not think!" She seemed dismayed at this.

"No matter, though it will make slaying Punpasay more difficult." I could take a knife from one of the sleeping guards.

They were slumped just around the corner, where a row of houses similar to my own stood. Could I release all those here? Would they run or had they accepted their fate? It would surely draw attention and just as surely most would be recaptured quickly.

On the other hand, a diversion of naked prisoners running for the gates could be an advantage to one disguised as a — what? Was this the costume of a priest?

My decision was made for me, for at that moment a priest, one even I could tell was of high status, came upon the scene. He looked to the warriors and then to Tamba and me.

"Miyawanagayun," he snarled. "Is this the lover you chose instead of me?" He was a soft, heavy-bodied fellow, one who indulged himself over much, perhaps.

The girl proved quick witted. "No, Holy One. I found the guards so and brought this man as quickly as I could." I knelt down as though examining them, so he could not look too closely upon my face. My disguise would not fool the man for long.

"What has happened to them?" he asked, standing above us. "Too much wine? They will lose their heads if that is so!" I found one of the men's knives, an obsidian blade, and slipped it into my hand before rising.

It was obvious that he recognized me at once so I had no choice but to plunge the blade into his thick neck. He only gurgled as he fell. Tamba and I looked down at the body, she clinging to my arm. "It is good," she whispered, and looked up at me with something akin to awe. That made me most uncomfortable.

But an idea presented itself. I pulled off Punpasay's collar and cap and replaced my own with them — a couple of small blood spots on the collar should not noticeable in the dark. Who would stop a high-ranking priest, off to an assignation with his woman? Past the ornately carved posts below Mihasa's altar we confidently strode, through the courtyard where a few worshipers stood and deferentially bowed to me, and out the great gates.

37. Escape

I remembered that Bato, the old Kohari we met in the Valley of Visions, had once escaped the temple. A fortuitous earthquake had saved his head, but he used that head and made sure to travel far from all Kohari lands after that, for every hand would have been turned against him — he belonged to Mihasa. Bato, in time, found his way over the mountains and into the service of Lord Hurasu.

We, too, should try for the mountains, but at this moment we stood on an island. Yes, it was a very large island and even had mountains of its own, but there were far too many Kohari dwelling here. We must cross to the mainland; our further course could be decided once we got there.

There are those among my people who can navigate anywhere, who make and understand maps made of string and sticks. I have not this skill. Once Marareta showed me how he drew a picture of the land, as seen by a bird flying higher than any that ever lived. Maybe the Kohari's Sun Bird could have such a view! From that map of his, though he told me he did not know how accurate it was, I knew a point stood out there across the water and that the shores of a bay curved away south of it, where fewer dwelt and the mountains lay close to the coast. We should make for it.

"Have you ever sailed, Tamba?" I asked.

"You mean go on the water, Hito?" There was great fear in her voice. "I could not."

"If you wish to live, you must." How had she thought we were going to escape? Fly away? No, that was harsh. Tamba had shown she was both brave and level-headed in getting me out of my captivity. That she feared the water was to be expected.

First I must find a boat for us. There were many on the beach beyond the temple gates, for the great shrine was built on a harbor. I knew little of sailing a Kohari boat and would prefer one of my accustomed dugout canoes. Not too small; we had a wide channel to cross.

There were canoes among the craft pulled up onto the sand, but they were not suited to the open water. Too small they were, and had no outriggers — the sort one might use on a river or around the shores of this lagoon. So we must steal a boat. It would be a matter of luck whether or not its owner was anywhere near by. That did seem unlikely in the middle of the night.

But a priest launching a boat in the dark would surely raise suspicions. I wandered along the line of vessels, my arm about Tamba to maintain the illusion we were lovers seeking privacy. Many of these boats, I could see, would be too large, too heavy, for me to launch on my own.

Launch I must, and soon, for surely Punpasay and the guards would soon be discovered. The alarms might be rising already. "This one," I whispered to my companion. It differed little from many of the others but its owner had left it halfway into the shallow waters. From laziness? Who could say. The boat was only slightly smaller than that of Wolak.

And we were well away from the torches of the temple compound now, amid a starry darkness. I began to push the boat off the sand. Tamba, too, put her shoulder to it and helped as she could. "We float," I whispered. "Get on board now." The girl looked at the boat's high sides, uncertain, so I picked her up by the waist so she might clamber over. With another push to make certain we were free of the bottom, I followed her into the craft.

None too soon, it seemed, for I saw torches further up the beach, moving about. I must get away from the shore, into the concealing night. Of oars, I knew little but I grasped them and clumsily paddled us out onto the still, dark water. Tamba peered toward the disappearing shore; soon, only the lights could be seen, flickering in the distance.

"Will they come after us?" she asked.

"They will, but boats leave no tracks to follow. We must be as far away as we can, as quickly as we can." I had little doubt the Kohari would guess we escaped onto the sea. When they found a boat missing they would be certain. That might not happen until dawn.

Would there were a breeze! Even the clumsy square sail would help get us further from this coast, get us on our way across the bay to the mainland. I continued to pull on the oars. "Are there any provisions on this boat?" I called to Tamba. "Look around and see what is here."

She rummaged about for a while. "What is this?" she asked, holding up a tangle of lines, hooks carved of shell at their ends. Of course, she would nothing of such things.

"They are to catch fish," I told her. "Are there any weapons? Any food?"

"There are many little fish in a basket. They do not smell good."

Bait. Probably too ripe for us to eat. "I have found a knife," she reported. Tamba sniffed at a leather bottle. "And palm wine." She shook it. "Not very much."

The moon was rising. It was not full but still cast light enough to worry me. Yet, I was glad of it for it showed me which direction was east. I rowed the opposite way.

"Oh, Hito," moaned Tamba, "my stomach does not like this!" We were rising and falling on larger swells now, evidence that we were out into the channel between island and the still distant mainland coast. I should try to steer us more southerly, away from the heavily populated areas.

A breeze arose at last, as did our sail, and we wallowed along, the dawn behind us and still far-off mountains ahead, their crests touched with gold.

38. The Bay

Had Tamba all this in mind when first she came to visit me? I suspected she been scheming for some time. Perhaps, even, Punpasay wasn't quite the evil man she implied. She was schooled in intrigue, this young woman.

Ah, I had cast the dice she handed me. What other choice had I? We drew closer to the coast all that day, but angled southward rather than landing. The further we went, the fewer villages might be found. It would be best to land at night, as well, wouldn't it?

I decided otherwise once we drew closer. The shore was becoming rocky and hazardous. "Why do you turn back to the sea?" wondered Tamba as I adjusted our course. There was barely controlled fear there.

"I think it best we get well away from the coast and stay at sea tonight. Then I shall try to land at dawn when I can see what I am doing." Once the moon rose, I should be able to navigate enough to keep us from coming too close to shore. I looked up and hoped those clouds would not close in.

That might be something to petition Teva about, might it not? Surely a god of rain could move the clouds about.

And perhaps as a god of love, Teva had put this comely girl at my side. A Kohari girl — surely that was not meant to be. Nor was it something to pursue at that moment.

Teva did not remove the clouds. Moreover, he caused them to rain on us. I had no way to anchor so I could only attempt to keep this boat headed away from that unseen shore, moving as slowly and cautiously as possible. By midnight it had cleared and I could see my way once more.

No mountains appeared at all. I must have been too careful, kept us too far eastward. Tamba stared at the water all around us. "The coast is over there somewhere," I said, pointing to the west. "It is better to be too far away from it than too close."

"It will only be close enough when my feet are on it," she responded, and attempted to vomit again. There was nothing left in the girl. "So this is how Bagap punishes the wicked!"

"He is only encouraging you to feed his minions," I informed her. Tamba laughed weakly. I was glad to see she could do that.

The shore was visible by dawn. Rain had returned, misting the mountains that rose behind. I thought this a good thing, in all. It gave us more cover. A beach was what I needed, but one not too close to a village.

I steered the clumsy boat in closer, scanning for a landing spot as we continued down the coast. Not there; several huts rose beyond a beckoning harbor. It was to be hoped no one had noticed this lone vessel passing by.

A little point, all rocks — there was no beach on the other side but it was sheltered from the waves. I could drive this boat right up onto the shore. What matter if the rocks tore out its bottom? Best it be destroyed and leave no sign that we had landed here. I adjusted the sail and headed us in.

"Whatever you wish to carry with you, get it now," I ordered, "and be ready to jump." Tamba would not be able to swim, I was quite certain. I would have to stay near her.

A moment later we came to a sudden stop. The boat groaned against the rocks. "There," I pointed. "I shall go first." For me, it was barely a jump at all, only a long step to one of the rounded dun rocks that rose from the water. I turned, planting my feet, and held out my arms. "Jump!" Her eyes were wide and fearful, but Tamba did not hesitate, not a second. Then she was in my arms and being carried to land through thigh-deep shallows. I do not believe she even got wet.

I looked back to our boat. It rested, listing, on the rocks. It could sink no deeper, not unless it were somehow dislodged by surf or wind. That was not in my control. "I'm hungry," said Tamba.

So was I. I could even wish for some kuru at that moment. "We won't find any food here," I told her. "Let's go."

Go into the mountains. There was no other choice.

39. Choices

We could not remain in Kohari lands, that was certain, and the only way home was to cross these high peaks. My home, that is. Where might Tamba wish to go?

"With you," was the answer she gave me. Perhaps that was her only choice, truly.

It was not an uninhabited land; we came, more than once, unexpectedly on a patch of cleared land, a hut. We did not make ourselves known but we did help ourselves to anything that was ripe. Kuru should be baked so we took none of that. I was not prepared to risk a fire. Nor was I sure I could start one in the light but persistent rain.

Up forested valleys we climbed. This was most ill-advised, I knew, to head into the mountains without provisions, without warm clothing, without even weapons. We must rest and plan when we were sufficiently far from men.

Indeed, we could probably find someplace up there where we could remain as long as we lived. Would that be so bad, to have a secluded hut, with Tamba at my side and, in time, children? I regarded the Kohari woman trudging at my side. No, she could not live that way nor would I ask her. I did not even know if she wished to remain with me, once we were safe.

Nor, for that matter, if I wished to remain with her. I had made no advances. As attractive, as desirable, as this dancer was, I was not even sure I liked her very much.

There was a hollow in the rocks, not a deep cave that might harbor bats or worse, but enough of a depression to give us cover from the weather. We had climbed for six days. "This would be a good place to make a camp," I said.

We were not yet that high. This valley was lush, warm. We could gather ourselves here for a while before moving on. All this I explained to Tamba. "And then we go over the mountains?" she asked.

I nodded. If we can, I thought. I was not sure of that. "Are your people on the other side?" Tamba turned her eyes to the peaks.

"Hmm. Not here, I think." The Mora homeland was surely further south, wasn't it? "I think if we cross here we might come to the great River Gurang."

"Oh, I have heard of it! It is full of crocodiles longer than the biggest boat!"

"Not where we would meet it." I hoped. "I think we could reach its upper waters if we can find a pass." That would be the hard part. Crossing the mountains further north would be easier, for they were both lower and, I was certain, not so wide. But that would bring us out on a rocky uninhabited coast, the one I had sped past in the boat of Bohasuk.

"I must fashion a spear," I went on. "We could use both meat and furs." A sharpened stick would have to do, at least for now. Or could I attach one of our knives to a shaft? No, too great a chance of losing them. My wooden point could be hardened by fire.

Which I went about building right then. It turned out this was something of which Tamba was knowledgeable and soon the two of us had a blaze going. I think we both felt better about things once we sat by that flame, that we had accomplished something, that things would somehow turn out right.

Two days passed. I managed to bring down some small game, even a sort of deer I did not know, but standing no higher than my waist, and we ate well at last. I skinned out any animal I took, for we would need the protection of leather and fur in the mountains. Tamba was intrigued by this, never having seen it done nor even knowing that it *was* done.

Tamba did not stray from our base. I gave her strict warnings about this — she did not know the world and would certainly become lost. Nor had she any skills to help me in the jungle. She would not recognize any edible fruit that grew wild.

And as we relaxed, our minds turned to something other than survival. Mine did, at least. I found myself watching the Kohari dancer and found myself wanting her. Ah, but no. It would not do, not now, and especially with her never having been with a man.

It did not help when she slept close to me that night, when I awoke with her arms wrapped around me. Carefully, I disengaged them so as not to awaken her, and sat up. Before me stood Bohasuk, his young followers arrayed behind him.

"So, Mora, do I take your head now or return you in bonds to the temple?" he growled.

"Kill him," called one of the boys. Tamba was awake by now and stared wide-eyed at them.

"There is more honor in taking him back alive," the nobleman told him. "More prestige." He returned his baleful gaze to my face.

"And this was a personal insult to me, after I brought you before Mihasa. I *will* see you die on her altar!"

What could I say? I had never expected such a pursuit. I had vastly underestimated this man, thinking him all bluster. He must have hurried after me immediately, with these young warriors he had at hand.

"We saw your boat," Bohasuk continued. "From there it was not so hard to track you. Did you actually think to go over the mountains, dog?"

"I have done it before."

He clearly did not believe me. Bohasuk was the sort who could not be convinced of anything he did not already believe.

"What of the girl?" asked another young man. I could tell what he was hoping and wished to throttle him.

"Tell me, Hito of the Mora," sneered Bohasuk. "Should I give her to my followers? No?" He laughed mockingly. "Give your word not to try to escape again and they will not touch her. Otherwise, they will have both her and her head."

What choice had I? "I give my word, Lord Bohasuk"

"It is good, then." He leered at Tamba for a moment. "I think I want her as my own. She can be one of my concubines." He told the girl, "You know you will be slain if you are returned to the temple and your head will join that of this Mora."

"As you wish, my lord," she meekly replied.

Tamba, too, had no other choice.

40. A Duel

We began our march back toward the coast almost immediately. Six warriors had Bohasuk with him, none of them much more than a boy and some of them definitely boys. I am not sure any of them were even as old as Tamba.

Why had the noble Kohari taken these youths adventuring, rather than more seasoned men? Perhaps it was intended as a rite of passage for them, before they could join his warriors. Or maybe he could more easily impress them and enjoyed their adulation. This question was never answered for me.

Half a day we descended toward the distant sea. How many more would pass before I was again at the temple? How many until my head was removed from my shoulders? I had little hope of escaping once I was returned, but my oath to Bohasuk would no longer apply when I was out of his custody. Empty dreams of finding his house and rescuing Tamba came and went as I trudged wearily on.

A war cry erupted. Men, Kohari warriors, sprang from ambush. Not so many, were they? Four? But they were warriors, not boys. And before us stood Lord Hidlat, brandishing a knobbed war-club. "Face my challenge, Bohasuk!" he roared.

Bohasuk charged, his heavy spear ready to pierce his enemy. No, he changed his grip at the last moment and used it as a staff, striking with the butt at his opponent. Hidlat deflected the blow easily with his oblong shield. A swing of the club; Bohasuk jumped back beyond its arc.

The two stood glaring at each other. Bohasuk rose nearly a head taller than his adversary, and was a man of broad shoulders and powerful arms. The squat Hidlat had massive legs and thick muscular forearms. I would not want to wrestle Lord Hidlat; his grip would not be broken. My eyes flickered to the rest of the battle to see it already over. Four of Bohasuk's men lay on the ground; the other two were prisoners.

A thrust from Bohasuk was turned away and now Hidlat did not swing his weapon but drove it straight into Bohasuk's abdomen. Only the thick armor of crocodile hide the man wore saved him. Thrust, parry, attack — so it went on, longer than almost any duel I had ever seen. More typically, one man quickly overwhelms the other.

Then, as Bohasuk again stabbed in with his spear, Hidlat's tactic changed. He used not his club, but let it dangle from his wrist on its thong as he grabbed the larger man's arm and pulled him in, and put his knee into him. A moment later, Bohasuk was on the ground and a moment more his brains were scattered by Hidlat's club.

Hidlat turned to see the two prisoners his men held. "It is too far to take them back," he decided. Without more discussion, their heads were hewn from their bodies with flint-edged swords. At least the boys died bravely, making not a sound, showing no fear, when the blows came. Then those already slain were accorded the same treatment. The Kohari leader spoke at last to me.

"You I did not care about, neither to rescue you nor to return you to the temple." He considered that. "I should take you back, for you are Mihasa's.

"It was Bohasuk I followed and Bohasuk I wanted. We had old scores to settle." Hidlat casually kicked the body lying at his feet. "Someone make sure to get his head," he ordered.

Tamba and I stood, uncertain of our fates, as Hidlat's men went about their business. When all was done, he regarded us for a moment and then turned his back to us, saying, "I see no one here. Let us go." His men followed him down the trail, bearing seven heads but leaving the bodies behind.

They had not stripped those bodies, I saw. We might as well take their weapons and clothing ourselves. Had Hidlat meant it to be so or did they simply not care?

Tamba stood and watched me methodically remove anything of value. Every piece of bark cloth could be useful, and every flint or quartz blade. All the spears? I might as well; it was not so far to carry them back to our camp. I picked up one ax I might find useful but left the others and the war-clubs lying.

There remained only a few bits of jewelry. No earrings, obviously! "Would you like any of the ornaments, Tamba?" I called. She shook her head with considerable vigor. Robbing the dead was apparently not acceptable.

We headed back up the valley in silence. At last, my companion spoke. "I would have gone with Bohasuk and never complained. It might not have been a bad life." She sniffled. "I would have let you go to your death and forgotten you, even though you saved me. Twice."

"What else could you have done?" I asked.

Her expression grew fierce. "Slip a knife into Bohasuk when he came to me." She looked up me. "I might have done it!"

"So you might." But I doubted it. Tamba preferred survival.

41. Making Ready

Now must we prepare for the mountains. I had decent spears at last for the hunting. Not ideal, for they were heavier war-spears and had not the proper balance for long throws. Several knife blades augmented our two. I still needed to prepare furs — I remembered well the bitter cold of the high mountains. We Mora had not known of nor expected that, but Marareta had made sure we had what was needed.

The seven bark-cloth kilts could certainly help. I was not surprised that Tamba was skilled with a needle, and had some among the meager belongings she had brought from the temple. It was to be assumed that the dancers would know how to make costumes.

But did we truly need to enter the peaks? I spoke of this to the girl. "We could wait a few seasons here and then make it back to the coast," I suggested. "Perhaps I could find a boat and sail us to my homeland." It was a dangerous plan but was it more dangerous than crossing the mountains?

"No!" She was quite adamant. "I will not go on the water again!"

I had to smile. "We Mora love the water. If you come to live among us you will not be able to avoid it."

Tamba considered that. "Maybe a small pool, such as we bathe in at the temple."

"I live beside a rather large lake," I told her. "That is where I wash."

"Lake? That is like a pool?"

How could I explain it? "Larger than a pool but smaller than the sea," I said. "Big enough for boats but the water is fresh, not salty."

"Like a river." She thought she understood.

"But the water does not move."

"Oh. If you say so, Hito."

The water did move in A'auwa, being a part of the Teoma's flow, but I did not wish to complicate matters. When she saw the lake she would understand.

Would she see A'auwa one day? I did not even know if I would again behold it. A part of me yearned to be there, to sit and drink wine at the shrine of Teva. But could Tamba, a woman of the Kohari, belong there, where she had no status?

I had also Bohasuk's crocodile-hide armor. It fit me well but I knew it was too heavy to wear across the mountains, even if it might protect me against dangers there. If Bohasuk had also worn a helmet of it the Kohari might even still be alive, but a tall crown of bark-cloth had been on his head, an emblem of his status but offering no protection.

We needed boots, this I knew. We were used to going barefoot, both of us, or donning sandals if we must. But this too was something that was necessary in the high mountains. That thick crocodile hide might better be used to protect our feet. It was with reluctance that I cut it into usable pieces.

I dried meat, or attempted it. The damp air worked against me in this, as it did in the curing of animal skins. Yet I managed to make enough eventually, as much as we could carry and still walk!

How long did we linger in that little cave? I lost track. I admit it.

Less than a season but perhaps not much less. And Tamba and I looked upon each other many times, knowing what would come but neither willing to initiate it.

It would be unwise, would it not? said one part of me. Best to wait. No, said another voice, what if you perish in the mountains, one or both, never knowing the other's love? Maybe Tamba had voices like that too.

The time neared to leave. We lay side by side in the night, shoulder to shoulder, the small fire crackling before us, neither yet ready to sleep.

Tamba turned to face me, the shadows cast by the flames dancing on her face. "I shall never again dance at the temple," she whispered. "There is no need to remain calansa."

It would mark the final break with her former life. "Is this what you wish?"

"Yes, Hito of the Mora. I want you. All of you."

"And I, you, my Tamba."

So it was, as I took her in my arms and we first made love. And all was ready for us to walk together into the mountains on the morrow.

42. *Finding a Way*

If I could find a good-sized stream, even a river, that might be the best route upward. The one that flowed in this little valley was barely a trickle — it would lead us nowhere. So we must backtrack, search out some better way.

The proper direction, of course, was south. I knew that I might just as readily have found our path to the north, but I did not wish to travel deeper into Kohari lands, towards more populous areas. I also knew that any large stream would be likely to have inhabitants along its banks. That we must risk.

Many streams we did cross. Perhaps any one of them might have done but I felt that the further south we went before attempting the mountains, the better. Not too far or we might find ourselves crossing into the Valley of Visions! At last, I decided one was suitable, a wide but shallow flow, swiftly running and riddled with rocks. No canoe could travel there. "Your people are less likely to build their houses by such a river," I told Tamba. She took my word for it.

No villages did we see, nor even solitary huts, as we followed that valley upward. Nights we spent in each other's arms, no longer fearing, no longer holding back. We loved, if only for a time. Who could see what the future held?

Yes, I loved Tamba then, even knowing how fragile that love might prove, how unsuited we might truly be to each other. That she was manipulative and cunning I had recognized almost from the start. As she had used me, I too had made use of her. Who might say whether either of us would still breathe had it been otherwise?

It was far up, where the air began to grow cool, that we came upon a rambling house built of thatch and bamboo, set, almost concealed, among spreading fig trees. A pen, I could see, with pigs, and chickens scratched before its entry. A woman, too, stood there and had spied us. "We might as well make ourselves known," I told my traveling companion. "I think we are far enough away from things to need not fear."

She clung to my arm and whispered, "I love you, my Hito, but it would be good to speak with someone else for a change." I was unsure whether she teased or spoke in earnest, but, either way, she was right.

The woman seemed unnerved by our approach, almost as if she wondered whether it might be best to turn and run. Instead, she called out loudly. A name, she called. I saw a child poke its head from the hut's entry and disappear again. Moments later a man appeared on the other side of the clearing, holding a spear.

I would be cautious too, at the approach of strangers in so remote a place. Yet we were only a pair, and one a woman. There was little reason to fear us. As he approached, the man addressed us in Kohari.

A word or two I caught, but most I could not understand. I knew not his dialect. In the pidgin, I replied but the fellow only seemed puzzled and shook his head. He was not a big man, and lean as twisted leather, a man scraping out a life here at the edge of the mountains. I held up both my hands to sign that I meant no mischief to him or his family.

Tamba stepped forward and spoke in her native dialect. Where had she been born among the scattered Kohari tribes? I had never asked her of this nor how she had been chosen for the temple. There seemed to be some mutual understanding here, and the two carried on a halting conversation. Little sense could I make of it, yet it ended with us being invited into this family's home.

There were a number of children, some nearly grown, one still at its mother's breast. Agetap, our host named himself. Never did I learn the names of the others in that house. They might have been told to Tamba.

"They are like us," the girl informed me. "Agetap fled here and hid from men. He does not say why." Tamba would have enough sense not to pry further. "I shall tell him we are the same." She narrowed her eyes at me. "He can see you are no Kohari but I think he cares not."

I attempted to thank our hosts for their hospitality. Perhaps they understood enough of the words in the pidgin to catch my meaning, or perhaps my tone was enough. We ate with Agetap and his family and I was pleased to see no kuru whatsoever.

So this Kohari had exiled himself here, he and his family. Had those youngsters ever known other humans? They would want to leave someday, to find spouses, to build houses of their own. Surely the world had forgotten Agetap and whatever transgression he might have committed. Surely, it was safe to again mingle with other men. But fear is a relentless master, and a hard one.

Tamba spoke with them late into the night, a conversation I

could not follow nor even understand. I went to sleep on the mat provided and let them go on. Later, the girl snuggled in beside me — it was cool enough here when the sun fell below the mountains that we needed a cover. "Agetap asks if we would like to live here." She giggled. "We would be a village!"

Had not I thought of such a thing, some time ago, and dismissed the idea? "Would you want this, Tamba?" I asked.

She was silent for a long time. I thought maybe the girl had fallen asleep. "It is not for us," she at last replied. "Even if we might think so, at first."

That, perhaps, was the wisest thing I had ever heard Tamba say.

43. Wanderers

It was so that I had never spoken with Tamba of her past, though I had told her many tales of my own. But those were heroic tales, of battle and journey, not of my early days. And so I spoke. "I grew up even poorer than Agetap and his family," I told her. "My father died when I was yet a small child, leaving us without wealth or land." I stopped and looked down the valley toward the roof of Agetap's house, distant now, almost hidden among the trees, before continuing. "My mother's family provided for us, as is custom, but we were not truly welcome in their houses. I chose a warrior's life as soon as I was able." For a moment, I stood silently. "My mother died not long after I left." I had always felt some pain over that, even knowing I had nothing to do with it.

Tamba had listened to all this patiently. "I will pray to Lugan for her spirit," she vowed. "I do not know if my mother lives. My father was a wealthy farmer, in the north, and I the daughter of one of his concubines. He sold me when I was only six to the trainers of dancers." She spoke as if this were the ordinary course of things. "Had I shown no talent, I would have ended up a servant. Or worse." That was motivation to train hard.

We resumed our trek toward the mountains. There was no need to hurry and I took time to hunt during those days, rather than use the meat I had cured. We must make sure we would have enough food when we wandered among those peaks. Finding a pass could take days or seasons, if we had the luck to find one at all. This I knew but did not tell Tamba.

But I thought I had done well in choosing this stream, although it dwindled day by day. There did not seem to be much rain here, high up. Perhaps as in the Valley of Visions — Marareta had explained this to me — the mountains shut out much of what came in from the sea, far to our west.

The trees became those that bear cones as we went on, not the tall firs I have seen in other high places, but stunted pines. Game was sparse, and hid in burrows on the steep, rocky hillsides. Yet we still had a clear and not overly difficult way.

At last, that way must be abandoned, and another path over the mountains found, for it turned away from the peaks. We tried many; some proved to be blind ways, impassible, leading nowhere, and we must turn around and try another. But slowly we did draw nearer the heights.

Not yet too cold was it, at least during the days. At night, we were thankful for the furs we had carried. I knew how bitter it might be at the top of the mountains, where water became like sand. Maybe it would not be so bad here; I knew these peaks did not rise quite so high as those I had before crossed.

Ah, those nights! Those too I had remembered, how the stars shone so brightly, so seemingly close that one would think he could reach out and pluck them. The gems on Tamba's necklace were as nothing beside them; they did not deserve the name of 'star-stone.'

And now Tamba beside me to see them. There were no complaints from the dancer; she was disciplined, better trained than many a warrior. Beneath that sky, I would speak of my homeland, of all that might be on my return. I spoke of A'auwa and of the Great Falls and those of Pana'a, and of the great houses of the kings. I spoke of the groves where stood the shrine of Teva.

Yet I spoke not of ambitions nor wealth, nor even of marriage, only of solid things, things one might see and hold, as I held Tamba. Of those other things, I tried not even to think. They were too complicated.

Up another valley we trudged, low cliffs rising on either side of a rubble-choked way. Gray and dun was it, with a pale sun in a deep blue sky standing over all. A harsh cry sounded above our heads.

Along the steep cliffs, on ledges and outcroppings, were nest after nest, made of piled high branches. On those nests were griffins, many griffins, and their young, squawking, crying, demanding constant feeding. We had wandered into a rookery.

44. Valleys

I had known griffins, both wild and those kept in Hurasu's fortress of Ten Sarac, High Sanctuary. There they were ridden by his messengers and scouts, boys and girls many of them, for the beast-birds could not bear a greater weight far.

As things normally go, even a griffin of the largest breeds will not attack a human, much less two of them. We are bigger than the game they usually hunt, the goats of the mountains, the small antelope of the savannas, and they have learned, too, that we can fight back. Griffins can not be considered particularly bright, but they can be taught.

I could see the tawny coats of fine feathers, almost a downy fur, the dark ruffs about their necks, the cruel curved beaks that can rend flesh like an obsidian blade. I could see also that they were upset by this intrusion. We were much too close to their nests.

So similar was the color of their coats to the rocky walls that we might have passed by without noticing them, had it not been for the cries of the young. Tamba only stared at the creatures, unbelieving, unable to move. "Slowly," I whispered to her. "We must get away from here. And do not look at them!" To turn our eyes on the great birds could further upset them. If we seemed to ignore them, they might ignore us.

But for once, Tamba's discipline could not hold. She cried out and began to run in terror. Blindly, she ran, and it took her even closer to one of the nests. I saw the griffin launch itself, to attack this threat. A female — they were smaller, more lightly built, and their ruff was not so full and dark.

Still dangerous, and more so for a panicked girl with no thought but to run far away. I dashed after her, spear at the ready. I would not think to throw it; if I managed to hit my target, it would probably only enrage the griffin and I would be without weapon. I must reach Tamba first.

Fortunately, it did not immediately stoop upon her as it might if it were hunting. The instinct was to defend the nest. It hovered, assessing this intruder and crying out a challenge, as Tamba stumbled on, more slowly now. Then I was between them, more or less, and could attempt to frighten the creature away. Or, if necessary, fight it. I stretched out my arms, so I might seem larger, and stood still. For a moment it regarded me with fierce eyes, the wide wings flapping, then wheeled back to it nest and young — satisfied, perhaps, that it had dealt with the threat.

Tamba stood still now, her chest heaving. There was no sense in scolding her. What did she know of griffins? Yet she stiffened when I took her in my arms, perhaps feeling shame for her lapse. We said nothing but went onward.

There are worse dangers than griffins in the high mountains. Bears dwelt there, and dragons. But worse yet are the avalanches that might sweep one away. These one does not see coming. They give no warning until they come roaring toward one. Many we heard or saw at a distance and tried to avoid going that direction. Some came closer, so close we must take shelter behind a standing rock or outcropping as pieces of the mountains came bouncing by.

And onward we went, up one valley and then another, over low ridges and some not so low, seeking a way. I could not show Tamba how discouraged I was. Were we going the wrong direction, coming no closer to a way between the peaks? Were we wandering, lost?

The next valley we entered was wider, a bit more hospitable in appearance. There was even vegetation clinging to the slopes. I did not know if that was a good thing. Had we become turned around and descended? At least we could camp more comfortably here tonight, I told myself. I might even be able to hunt up a marmot or other denizen of the high country.

"We shall stay here tonight," I decided. "What do you think, Tamba?" I added. I should remember to ask her, even though she never opposed my choices.

"Anywhere, Hito," came her listless reply.

I found a good spot, one relatively sheltered from the winds, and started to unpack our gear. Suddenly, we were surrounded by small, naked, hairless men and women, brandishing spears.

"Poto!" Tamba exclaimed. "They are real!"

45. The Poto

Ot-Ob-Oh is what the beast-men of the Shrouded Valley call them. Hurasu referred to them as Fay. Marareta had named them with one of those hard-edged words from his own language. I will not attempt to say it for you.

Tamba seemingly had another name for them. "The Kohari know of these people?" I asked her.

"They eat bad girls!" she wailed. "My mother told me this!"

"Then you are safe," I reassured her. "In truth, I have met these Poto before and had dealings with them."

I first attempted to greet them in the pidgin. Some of them squinted at me as though they recognized some of the words, but they only jabbered at each other in their tongue, unwilling to acknowledge it. I had heard that language before but spoke it not. The looks they continued to give us were unfriendly.

It had been long since I had spoken Zikem, the language we learned in the Valley of Visions, but I attempted it now. Ah, this they understood, at least some of them, at least some of the words. They chattered excitedly among themselves when I used this tongue, turning their pinched faces toward me and then back to their comrades. One approached and addressed me, almost deferentially. "You are a servant of the Lord of Visions?" he asked.

"I am his friend," I replied. "I have served him in the past." That was true. I had been in his army.

He considered this, then looked up at me with beady eyes set close on either side of a long nose. "Feel free to remain here tonight. None of our people will molest you."

"I thank you. And I thank your queen." I knew this folk was ruled by women and undoubtedly one of those standing about held that office. How could one tell when all went without clothing? The little fellow seemed surprised I would know this.

Tamba had recovered from her fright and now peered at the Poto with some curiosity. "They are not going to eat us?" she asked, almost whispering. The girl still sounded doubtful.

"Not today," I told her. "My friends and I met other tribes of their people further south and they showed us a way through the mountains. Perhaps we can learn of one from these, um, Poto." I might as well just call them that.

"That would be good, Hito," she felt. "They are very small," Tamba continued, looking again at the Poto.

"Yes, small," I agreed. Most came to around my waist in height. Many had disappeared by now, back to their underground homes, but three remained, maybe set to watch us.

"But, ah, not everywhere," she said, contemplating the naked male closest to us. This was also true.

I had to laugh. "They are ugly though, you must admit." This I said in a near whisper, just in case one or another of them actually did understand the pidgin.

"They probably think the same of us. A pair of ugly giants!"

Maybe so. Maybe we frightened them as much as they had frightened Tamba. But they were many and we were only two. Had I gone to my weapons when they appeared, the little people might

169

readily have slain us.

One of the Poto approached us again. The same with which I had spoken before? I thought so but can not be certain. "We bring you fire," he said, holding out a stone bowl. Embers glowed within it.

"You are gracious," I said, taking it. A blaze would indeed be welcome this night.

Tamba looked over my shoulder. "Oh. I shall gather some wood." Off she went.

"She is not known to the Lord of Visions, is she?" asked the little man. "She looks like those who live below us."

"She would be of that people. We escaped enemies there and hoped to go over the mountains and far away."

"These are our mountains," he stated with considerable gravity. "We do not like intruders. Had you not spoken to us in Zikem, we would surely have killed and eaten you."

Best I not tell Tamba of this.

Part IV. The Rain

46. From Afar

"We have spoken from afar with the Lord of the Valley," said the Poto woman. I much suspected she was their queen. I knew that the little people had this ability, all of them, to speak as did Hurasu and Oorto, though none had anything approaching their power.

"And he knew me?" I asked. Let us hope Hurasu had not become forgetful — he was over three thousand years old, after all.

"He did, Hito of the Mora. He seemed amused but not surprised that you had a female companion." Perhaps she was a bit amused as well. "It is good to have powerful friends."

I could not disagree with that. "And we would have Hurasu as our friend so we shall aid you," she went on. "Not all my people think this is wise."

Some, then, remained inimical toward me. I was aware the Lord Hurasu was not universally loved among the Poto. "I would seek a favor of you, my lady. Could you ask the Vision Lord to speak afar to my friends and let them know I live?"

She squinted up at me. "I would suspect he has done so already but we shall do as you ask."

"Then we should be on our way and bother your folk no more."

Nor tempt those who might be hungry. "Are we far from a pass?"

"There are many passes, some easier of crossing than others. And some, I think, would not take you where you wish to go." She laughed at my expression, though I had attempted to hide my annoyance. The Poto laugh no differently than we and seem to find the same things humorous. "I myself shall lead you to a good place to cross. There are those nearer but, as I said, they would not take you where you wish to go."

The sun was already climbing high. "When, my lady?"

"Now. Gather your things." That was satisfactory.

"We are leaving," I called to Tamba. "We have guides."

"They are to be trusted?" she asked, eyeing the Poto queen.

"I think so. And we have no choice." A shrill whistle sounded. I looked about to see every Poto had disappeared. A shadow passed over me and I peered skyward to see a griffin, wheeling and then heading off toward the east. "I would guess that griffins eat the Poto," I said.

"Everything eats something else," came her reply. "I'll get our packs."

The queen and a male would accompany us. Their names I can not tell you for they do not share them with outsiders. This time I was sure it was not the Poto with whom I had spoken before; I am not certain this one could even speak Zikem. He never said a word to me, only speaking their own language with his queen.

Up and down we went, but remaining on the east side of the mountains. For some time, we followed a long valley that ran between two high ridges. I saw a smoking peak off to our west, one of the many volcanoes in the mountain chain. Some of those we Mora knew and had named. I knew not whether this was one of them.

It seemed odd to huddle together with these little people at night, sleeping close for warmth. Maybe they should take to wearing some warm clothes! Once the queen whispered as we lay there, "The woman is your lover?"

"She is," I said. Tamba, of course, could not understand our speech.

"But I have not seen you copulate. Is she angry with you?"

How to answer such a question? "It does not seem appropriate with you here."

"I do not understand. Did you think I would feel left out?" Her dark beady eyes regarded me. "I could join in if you desired."

Aiee! "We, um, our people prefer privacy for this." I had enough sense to leave it at this, though all sort of questions went through my mind.

The next day she told me that her companion had spoken with Hurasu. Apparently the little man was the shaman of their tribe and better at such things than most. "The Lord of the Valley has spoken to your friend," she stated, and then turned and spoke a few words to the other Poto. "Oorto. That is the name. We could speak with this man directly but prefer to remain —" she searched a moment for a word, "hidden."

"I understand this," I replied, "and thank you once again."

We journeyed on that day. "Is this all your realm?" I asked the queen.

"It belongs to no one," came the answer. "There are not many of my people in these mountains. More live to the south, where you met them." She looked about at the arid rocky landscape. "This is not really our world. We may leave some day." She looked up at me. "We know where doors may be found."

Of what she spoke I had not the slightest idea.

Three days more we traveled before turning and climbing toward the backbone of the mountains.

47. The Road

"I will accompany you for a short way on this side of the mountains," said the queen, as we stood looking back at the gap. I thought I could find this pass again from this side, recognize enough landmarks, but I would be lost once I crossed back over. Nor had I any desire to again go there.

But I had some idea where I was now. I could point myself south and find the upper reaches of the Gurang. "This is where you live?" asked Tamba.

"It is far yet to my home," I told her. "The way will be much easier now, however." Her necklace caught my eye.

"Could you tell me, my lady," I asked, holding the strand up so the Poto queen could see the stones, "If such gems are to be found around here?"

"I have seen them closer to where we dwell. This area I do not know so well." She gazed at the stones. "There are prettier jewels."

"That is so," I agreed. But not so useful.

By day's end, the Poto were ready to part with us. "Follow this valley," the queen said, "and the stream and it will take you where you wish to go." We were high yet in the mountains, in a narrow cleft. This small rush of water beside us was undoubtedly flowing toward the Gurang.

"I thank you once again my lady," I said. "Your companion as well." I bowed toward the little shaman.

"It was a welcome diversion," she replied. "Life can be weary in the heights. And we live exceedingly long, Hito of the Mora." She looked at Tamba. "Now you two can make love again." With that, the pair turned back toward their distant home.

Her last suggestion was not a bad one. Not at this moment, however. The valley broadened gradually as we followed it, but still remained more a chasm. It fell, too, and the stream fell with it, here and there joined by water trickling from the rock walls or falling from their tops. It was a damp, uncomfortable place to camp, but the way could not be walked in one day, nor even two.

Then the rushing Gurang lay before us, also between high walls, and our stream fell into it, flowing between what seemed a number of natural but conveniently-placed stones. I knew better; we had reached Hurasu's ancient road across the mountains. Soon, Tamba and I were traveling that road, heading downward, westward.

The road, I remembered, was not without its hazards. The mardagoru and the great bear roamed these slopes and cliffs. The griffin and even the dragon might cross the skies. The path itself could be perilous, a narrow track above a precipice, and a cold wind blew down from the heights.

"I am tired of walking," said Tamba, her voice very small. "Do the mountains ever end?"

"Some might say we are already out of them." I too was weary, or I might have spoken words of reassurance rather than answering so. "Ah, Tamba, do you wish to stop and rest a time?"

"What need, if we are already out of the mountains?"

I could not help smiling at the sarcasm in her voice. A sharp tongue had the girl, when she chose to use it. "It is days yet to reach land that lies flat," I told her. "Once you are among the mosquitoes and crocodiles of the Gurang's swamps, you may yearn for the cool high mountains."

"Never!" At the moment I felt much the same about it. Our way was looking less and less like an intentionally constructed road and more like an ordinary river bank. I knew we approached its end. The river grew wider, ran closer, even as we descended to it. Soon we would be at a level with the Gurang.

"It should not be long," I announced, "that we can throw away our boots."

"That, Hito, is the best thing you have said to me in many days. My feet do not like their prisons!"

"Nor mine. I hope never to wear them again." It would be good to throw aside everything except a simple loincloth. I glanced at my companion. It would be good to see her that way, as well. Pretty girls should not be covered up so!

Soon. A flock of small parrots flying above the water on the following day was a good sign. There was more green about us, trees here and there on the slopes, rushes at the water's edge. My heart was lifted; thoughts of home were in my head.

But I did not see Tamba in that home. Could she share my life? Could she be happy among the Mora?

Between low bluffs, we watched the setting sun cast red and gold lights upon the river, and shadows lengthened toward us. "Let us camp here," I said to Tamba. I squinted into the west again. What was that? But another shadow?

No, it moved. A man, coming toward us. I knew who it must be

long before I could make out his features.
    Oorto had come to greet us.

48. A Friend

"It is a friend," I reassured Tamba. The first of many she must meet in a new land. A new world for her.

"He does not look like you." She sounded doubtful about all of this.

"He is of another people, the Diwarna."

She nodded. "I have seen captives at the temple." Tamba again gazed at the approaching man. "They always seemed very brave."

They would. A Diwarna would remain impassive to the last.

I embraced the man when he reached us, unable to speak for a moment, so filled with emotions was I. Until that moment a part of me had remained a prisoner, an exile from my home and those I loved. Then introductions were made.

"Kohari?" he asked. Wrapped yet in her mountain garments, there was little to see of Tamba but her face. She could pass readily enough for a woman of the Mora with only that to go by. Her height betrayed her, it is true, and the lack of tattoos would make identification more easy if she were not so covered up.

But her speech would ever set her aside from the Mora, and her ignorance of our customs. A lifetime among us could not completely remedy that. "Yes," I answered. "She helped me escape the temple."

"Then I welcome you as a friend, Tamba," he said to the girl. "Have you a fire?"

She shook her head. We had eaten cold meals for many days.

More than many days. Without further words, Oorto knelt down and began the business of fire-making. Tamba looked on in curiosity for a moment, before saying to me, "We should gather wood."

There was driftwood enough along the margin of the Gurang and we filled our arms. I think she wanted the opportunity to speak with me, away from the Diwarna. "Is Oorto wealthy?" she asked.

"No. He is a shaman among his people."

"Ah." Tamba looked back toward our camp. "That is like a priest, is it not?" The woman had no reason to trust priests.

"In a way. But the Diwarna have no temples and their shamans live as they do."

That seemed to satisfy her. We returned and soon had a blaze going. "Hurasu told me you were coming," Oorto told me, as we sat and chewed strips of dried meat. Perhaps we might partake of something better as soon as the morrow. "So I came, though I had said I would not walk this road again. Word had already reached your friends of your escape. Kohari traders told them." I think there was the slightest of smiles as he added, "I know not whether they might have attempted to rescue you."

I liked to think they would have but would never ask them. "All is well in my homeland? And here?" I asked.

"As you left it." He thought on that for a little while before continuing. "For the most part. I took your pack back with me to Gordie. He was most interested in the bright stones you had gathered. They are of great value, he says, in the land from which he came."

"But little here."

"The Kohari might trade for them, he thinks." He let his eyes rest on Tamba. "They seem to like such things."

"Your pack?" Tamba asked me. She looked suspiciously at Oorto; maybe she thought he had stolen it.

"It was left in our camp when I fell into the river," I told her. I must give Oorto all that tale, in time, but not now.

"I searched for two days and then went to Gordie," said the Diwarna. "He sent out men then and found your tracks so we knew you survived. I should have waited longer."

"But then he would never have saved me from Punpasay," stated Tamba. "It was fated to be!"

Fate? Pana'a had scoffed at the idea, yet things did seem almost foreordained. Ah, perhaps all things seemed random when one was far enough away from them, seeing all that was and could be, as in the visions of the priestess. It is only when we are among them that we think they make sense, that one thing leads to another.

But to Tamba I said, "I think you are good at making your own fate, little one." She smiled broadly at that, though I am not sure she completely understood my meaning. It seemed a compliment and that was enough.

"It is a day to where we camped by the falls of the Gurang," spoke Oorto, then reconsidered. "Maybe a half-day more than that, if you are weary."

"We are," I admitted, and put my arm about Tamba. "But soon we shall find rest."

49. Names

The next day we cast aside the last of our furs, going on in loincloths, and finally discarding our crocodile-hide boots when we reached the falls. By then, most of my story had been heard by Oorto, as we marched along. I think maybe Tamba was a little jealous of how we old friends conversed, sometimes leaving her out, perhaps even forgetting she was with us.

"Will we see any of your water dragons here?" asked Tamba, her voice expressing both eagerness and apprehension. She looked in a direction where they could not possibly lurk, the shallow water above the falls.

"If we did they would be in the pool." Oorto pointed. "It is unlikely they will show themselves. And do not go near the water, Tamba," he warned her. "There are most definitely crocodiles in it."

I heard a hail, saw a man waving to us further down the riverbank. "That is Pahe," Oorto informed us. "I asked him to wait here." The two greeted each other with a deep embrace; I suddenly suspected there might be more than friendship between them.

Tamba more than suspected it. "Ah, they are lovers," she whispered. "I thought maybe Oorto did not care for women. There was no desire in his eyes when he looked upon me."

"You expect that from men?" I whispered back.

She stared at me as though my question was unbelievably foolish. "Of course, Hito. How could I not know I was desirable?"

"Many people do not know themselves at all," I responded.

"Shall we head on to the house of Lord Gordie?" asked Pahe.

Oorto looked to the sky. Then he looked to Tamba and me. "No, in the morning. We camp here tonight." That perhaps was best; we were not so tired but it might be good not to rush the Kohari girl toward a house full of strangers. Give her a night here to listen to the music of these falls, to see, to smell, this new world, before we traveled on. Oorto might understand this better than anyone.

Fortunately, Pahe had hunted and many of the provisions he had carried here remained. We ate better than — ah, I can not say how long. I could not remember my last good meal! The sky was clear that night, rainy season long past, and Tamba and I counted stars before falling asleep in each other's arms.

We saw no water dragons as we followed the river the next day and that after, though I did point out the occasional crocodile to Tamba. There was no need to tell her they were not man-eaters, was there? In time, we turned and passed through the forest and, as before, I felt I should pray there.

To whom? "This is my temple," I told Tamba. "It is higher and grander than any men might build." She looked up into the canopy but said nothing. Maybe she thought I was speaking foolishly again, yet she took my hand as we continued.

Then came higher, more open ground and on we went to the house of Gordie. "It is a good house," Tamba admitted, when she spied it. "He is a noble?"

"Of sorts. His wife is sister to Oorto."

"Hmm. I don't suppose he is looking for a second wife."

Though I recognized the spirit in which that was spoken, I chose to answer seriously. "The Diwarna do not allow multiple wives and Gordie would abide by that." Then I could not help adding, "Women of the Mora sometimes take more than one husband."

"Oh! That is a very good custom, Hito."

Gordie stood outside his house, alone, and greeted me as we approached. I turned to introduce Tamba, but she pushed by me. "My name is Miyawanagayun, Lord Gordie," she stated rather emphatically, "but Hito calls me Tamba." The girl glanced at me and smiled. "Either is acceptable."

"Or even Ranadi," I added. I remembered it from the temple.

"I suppose so," she agreed, slowly nodding. It had been some time since any called her that.

"That means 'sister,' doesn't it?" asked Gordie. "We are happy to welcome you as a sister."

"A new name for a new home," the Kohari woman said, as much to herself as anyone else. "Yes, that is a good idea. I shall be Ranadi from now on. To you, too," she informed me.

"I am bound to slip up," I told her. "You have long been Tamba to me." I hoped I was not expected to treat her as a sister also.

"Three times are permitted. Then you will have to be beaten if you do it again."

"Yes, my Lady Ta — er, Ranadi."

"Then, Ranadi, come in and meet Demba and Malee," said Gordie. "And welcome back, Friend Hito. We have much of which to speak."

50. A Meal

"I have sent messages that you are safely here," Gordie told me. "That you had escaped was already known."

"So Oorto has told me." I gazed out upon the wide, shallow river that flowed slowly past his house, carrying bits of debris from swamp and forest toward the Gurang. Its color was darker here than further up.

"Your sword awaits you at Marareta's house. It seems your friend Wolak brought it to the Great Falls. He was quite offended over the breach of hospitality that got you captured and did this as a matter of honor."

"He should be happy, then, to hear the man responsible for that breach no longer has a head."

"Your doing?"

"No. He had enemies among his own people." There was no need to say more. "My story is too long to tell now in its entirety."

"You'll have to get a storyteller to make up an epic about you. All our other friends seem to have one."

"I was always happy to be only the companion of heroes in those tales." Let Marareta and Aranu have their names sung across the land.

Gordie nodded. He was the sort to agree with the sentiment. "Let's go in and gather for a meal. Your Ranadi should be refreshed by now." We had left her in the custody of Demba.

"I hear there were also several copper nuggets in the pouch

Wolak returned," my companion said as we ambled toward his house.

"It is so. If you wish I shall tell you where I found them. I have no desire to go back." This was true. I had known it but had not before put it into words.

"That is understandable." We paused at the bottom of the steps leading to his front porch. "It would be good if you could actually show me. We shall not speak of that now. Ah, here come our girls."

Tamba-Ranadi was now in a longer kilt, such as Demba and Gordie often wore. Not quite so long as and looser than the skirt she had worn in the temple it was, but covering more than the loincloth in which she had arrived. She might feel more comfortable attired so.

She was holding little Malee in her arms. "Look, Hito," she crowed, rocking the child in her arms, perhaps a little too energetically. "I have not held a baby since I was —" The wide smile briefly slipped from her face. "Well, almost a baby myself."

Then returned the smile, perhaps even broader than before. "I must have many babies!"

Perhaps we could work on that later. I was hungry just then, so I followed our hosts to the side porch where a meal was laid out. A large man sat there, doing business with a bowl of beer, a man I recognized. "Taki! What do you here?"

Ranadi eyed him as he rose to greet me. "He is like a mountain!" she exclaimed.

"Friend Hito. It is good to see you." He glanced toward Gordie. "And thank you for many things. Sit with me."

I did, and Ranadi and Gordie beside me. 'Friend' he called me? That seemed odd. "I thought you were with the warriors of Mahutunoa," I said.

"I injured one of my fellows in a fight over a woman. It was a fair duel but I was dismissed anyway." He recounted this in a matter-of-fact manner. "So are things. But I remembered what you told me of the trade village and decided to come over the hills." He inclined his head respectfully toward Gordie. "Your friend has given me a position."

"It is useful to have a noble Mora as my representative in the village," Gordie told us. "And he has found something else he likes there."

"I have a wife now," the big man proclaimed. "Her name is Tala."

Another surprise that was, but not such a bad match, I realized. Tala was soft-spoken but strong of will. Had she not twice crossed over the high mountains? Maybe just the sort of woman Taki needed to guide him.

"Then I offer my congratulations, Friend Taki." I grinned at him. "But if ever you mistreat her, I shall come back and rub your face in the dirt."

He looked at me with raised eyebrows before we both roared out our laughter and turned to the feast.

51. Children

"Are there many the size of Taki in your homeland?" asked Ranadi, as we lay side by side in the dark, in the house of Gordie. We were making up for time lost in the mountains but one must rest occasionally.

"I know bigger men," I told her, "and smaller. I would be considered of ordinary height, I think."

"He is fat," she stated.

"So he is. I fear my people tend to grow wide as well as tall."

A giggle. Ranadi lay her head on my chest. "If his wife bears him children would they return to his home?"

"I would not think it." Ah, this would require some care in explanation. "Tala's father was Mora but her mother of the Diwarna. So she has no status in my homeland, nor would her children." I thought it best to add, "If she and Taki remain here, that may not matter."

"Is this true of my children too? And of me?" She had pulled away from me. I could just make out her form, propped up on one elbow, by the moonlight filtering into our chamber.

"There are ways to change this. You — or Tala, for that matter — could be adopted into a Mora family."

"Hmm. I would not mind having a new father. The one I was given was not so good."

"A mother would be needed as well," I told her, "to inherit status. But you must learn our language if you become Mora." It was up to me to teach her, I realized. That would be no easy task.

"We need no words right now," she whispered, and put her lips to mine.

Two days more we remained at Gordie's home, during which most of my adventures were related and the source of my sun-stone nuggets revealed. Gordie was most interested in this; he would have been interested in Ranadi's necklace as well had I told him what sort of stones they were. But of that I said nothing.

"I am going to the Gurang with some of my men," he announced at the dawning of the next day. "I would have preferred you come along, but know you wish to travel on. When you are ready, Taki can escort you to the trade village." Without much more of a farewell, he and perhaps a dozen men climbed into three long canoes and launched into the river. I do not know if Gordie actually wanted copper but he did want to know where it might be found.

I found Ranadi at breakfast with Demba, little Malee crawling about nearby. "We could leave right now, if you wish," I said to her.

"Oh, stay a little longer," begged Demba. "It is good to have you here, Ranadi, and Malee likes you. And my brother has already gone off again." Oorto had paddled away the previous day, back to his people.

I sat down with the two of them, and helped myself to some taro paste. It was more sour than I prefer. "You should tell Gordie you want to go and visit with Amirea. She would love to see you and compare offspring." The two close friends had borne children at about the same time, but far from each other.

Demba sighed. "It would be easier to get Amirea here." She turned to the Kohari girl. "You must promise to come back and visit. And —" There was a hesitation. "If you wish, you would always be welcome to live here."

Ranadi only gave her new friend a hug. As much as she might like Demba and Malee, I could not see her living in this house, far from most other humans. "I think we should go tomorrow, Hito," she said.

So it was we departed the next day, with Taki and a pair of warriors. Two canoes we took; were the Mora less weighty, one might have sufficed. There were trade goods, too, being carried to the village. "There is a store of goods waiting for you there," Taki informed me. "Lord Gordie owed you for your nets, and the colored stones he kept." I had nearly forgotten these things. They seemed of little importance now, but it would be good to return over the hills with something to show for all of this. Besides Ranadi!

Being on water of this sort did not seem to bother Ranadi. She seemed interested in all we passed by and chattered much about little as we went along. I suspected she was nervous, underneath, about this next step on our long journey, and about what lay beyond it.

In canoes, and then on foot, from jungle to grassy savanna, we traveled. One could not see the trade village from a distance, for it lay in a shallow bowl of a valley, but we came around a low hill and there it spread before us, the house of the Mora rising above the haphazardly-placed huts and pavilions, the spring-fed pond close at hand, mirroring a cloud-filled sky.

"There is a pool in which you may bathe," I whispered to Rana-di, "and not a crocodile anywhere near."

She surveyed the village. "It is not so large, is it?"

"No, and few actually dwell here. It is a place where traders come and go."

"Ah. It is like the temple, in some ways." A good comparison, I thought.

"Then let me take you to our high priestess," I said. "Do you intend to see Ma'are?" I asked Taki.

"Not right now," he grinned. "I have a wife waiting." The two warriors had already deserted us, probably off to find something to eat. They and Taki had hurriedly stowed their packs away in one of the huts.

So it was that Ranadi and I presented ourselves at the house of the Mora. It is to be noted that Ma'are and Heho had two children for the amusement of the Kohari dancer.

52. Home

Gordie had been generous. Perhaps too generous, for it was a great load to carry back across the hills. And of what did that load consist? Pots, for the most part, the work of Amlee and Tala and now, I had learned, apprentices. I knew these were much desired in the Mora lands. But they were heavy and fragile.

I shouldered my pack and started toward my homeland. Three days had we remained in the village, I preparing for the coming journey, Ranadi wandering and looking at the many wares offered, watching the potters and craftsmen, or staying with Ma'are and playing with her children, even teaching the older one some of the movements of her dances.

Ranadi's own education in my language began there too, for Heho and Ma'are spoke only Mora within their own walls. This they did for the sake of the children, so they would not grow up with the pidgin as their first tongue.

Now we accompanied a small party of traders south. Ranadi I asked to carry our provisions, while I shouldered the heavy load of pots, packed in straw, a tumpline across my forehead to bear some of the weight. I was not the only merchant so loaded down; the goods brought from the north usually outweighed those taken there.

There is little to see along that route, only grasslands stretching on either side, the occasional lone tree rising, patches of scrubby bushes. Ones mind wanders as one trudges along. That Ranadi's did, I could see. She was pensive, thinking perhaps of her future.

Light showers fell at times, harbingers of the season to come. In rain had I left the land of the Mora and in rain would I return. The hills that separated that land for those of the Diwarna rose steep on this northern side, as cliffs in many places. Toward the familiar cleft in those cliffs, the most traveled pass between our lands, we climbed.

"This is the last time you will need to go over any sort of mountain," I told Ramadi. "Even little ones like these."

"Unless I go visit Demba," she replied. 'I' she said, not 'we.' Things could turn out so, I knew, we both knew. Our paths might part in the land of the Mora. What had we to offer each other now?

My heart ached and I knew not why. "Home," I simply said when we stood in the gap and gazed northward. "It can be yours, too."

She stared out at the vista but did not speak. "Are you heading to Marihana?" asked one of our companions.

I nodded. It seemed the best route. "It would be good to put this heavy pack in the bottom of a canoe and float down the River Teire the rest of the way," I told him. And then where? The house of Marareta or further down Teoma to the Great Falls? I had not yet decided.

"That is so," the man agreed. "Your woman is tired." We spoke in Mora, so Ranadi was unlikely to understand much, if any, of our words. "Her legs are too short for so much walking!"

"I think we wore them off," I joked, and we continued our descent into the lands of the Mora.

"Will we go to your house now?" asked Ranadi after a time.

Where would that be? I no longer dwelt at the house of Arierona, though I might be welcome there and many other places. My mind went to the little house of Hoka, among the trees, though not my home either. What I answered was, "No, we would have to walk far overland with our packs to so do. We shall rest with friends before heading there."

"You spend much time in other people's houses, Hito of the Mora," she noted. "It is a good thing most of them like you."

"They will like you even more," I assured her. She knew that as the lie it was but said no more.

I had no canoe waiting at Marihana, there at the bend of the Tiere, but one of our companions offered us a place. Traders willingly help one another, even though they will turn around and bargain without mercy. We floated past the Blood Stone, that somber reddish marker that is said to be an object of power. I pointed it out, saying, "We could take that path and come to the house of the High King. I must take you there, one day."

"You know the king of all the Mora?" she asked, perhaps a little surprised. I had never mentioned Poneiva, apparently.

"Since he was a boy," I replied, and laughed. "The stories name me as the companion of heroes. Poneiva is one of them."

"But now you are the hero. Do not deny this, Hito. Everyone tells me so." She looked into the clear water beside our canoe. "Are there crocodiles here?"

"Only those who eat fish live in our rivers," I told her. "They do not harm humans, unless provoked."

"I have heard of them taking very small children," spoke our companion from his place in the stern. I had as well, but never from anyone who actually witnessed such a thing. "Only if they are in the water," he added.

"I will not allow my children to swim until they are as large as Taki!" declared Ranadi.

Soon huts and villages began to appear along our way, and fields and groves. This lifted my heart, to be among my people again. Ranadi was curious, asking question after question. "Oh, a kuru tree," she cried out as we passed one garden. "We must stop and pick some for you!"

"You must learn how to cook it first," was my reply. Ranadi knew nothing of how to prepare a meal, beyond placing meat on a stick and holding it over a fire. There had been no opportunity to learn more on our travels, nor did temple dancers learn of such things.

"I think there are many things I must learn, man of the Mora," was her reply.

53. An Empty House

Where Teire met Teoma, we must part with our traveling companion — and his canoe. He journeyed south; I could have changed my plan, gone up the river and on to A'auwa, but felt this was not the time for that. The house of Isa was up there, as well, where I had promised to return. That too could wait. We stepped out onto the opposite bank, shouldered our packs, and waved a farewell.

"This is a larger river," observed Ranadi.

"The largest that flows through our lands, yet dwarfed by the Gurang." I answered. "We shall follow it for a short distance." I had never walked this shore before, only passed it by, a canoe carrying me one direction or the other. It was rich land and there were many villages. Too many, maybe. Some of these people should go live in the emptier lands to the north and east.

They gave us barely a look. Some might have recognized Ranadi as a foreigner. The young men certainly noticed that she was a pretty girl. The old men too, most likely. It was not far to the village near the house of Marareta.

What of Mehetu when I arrived at that house, bringing along this young woman? She had said we would talk when I returned. That would be awkward now. No, I owed Mehetu nothing. And I owed Ranadi — what? My life, yes. We had both paid and repaid that debt; it was unlikely either would still breathe had it not been for the other. But I had brought her to a strange land and she was my responsibility.

There seemed little going on at Marareta's house when we arrived before it. One man reclined on the steps leading to the front porch. Was that —? Yes, the storyteller Ulani.

"Just the man for whom I was waiting," he spoke in greeting. "Now I shall be first to craft your epic." His eyes turned questioningly toward my companion. "This is girl who saved you or you saved or something of that sort?"

"Both would be true," I answered. "Ranadi, this would be Master Ulani."

"Not Master yet," he objected. "In time."

Ranadi knew Ulani by reputation. His name was mentioned from time to time in Gordie's house and at the trade village. "I am dwelling here for a season or two," he went on. "I shall have an apprentice."

"Toare," I guessed.

"Yes. He has chosen not to pledge himself as a warrior to Anana, now that he is at the age to do so. He will study with me for a while and then decide whether to be poet or warrior." He rose and stretched. "Not that he can not change his mind later. Marareta has promised him a place with his warriors if he chooses that path. All this, of course, is the taona's doing."

"Of course," I answered.

"Well, come along inside. Panoha is here somewhere but just about everyone else has gone."

Panoha was there, resting on the south-facing porch. That she was very near to delivering her child was obvious. I gave her my greeting in the pidgin, for the sake of Ranadi, and we continued to speak in that tongue. "My greetings to you, my lady Panoha. I present Ranadi to you."

The noblewoman acknowledged the girl with a nod. "Greetings, Hito," she said, giving me a weak smile. "Forgive me that I do not rise."

"The taona is not here?" I asked. It seemed strange for him to go away with his wife so near to giving birth.

"He has gone to see Samua, who is at the house of Arierona and unlikely to ever leave. He has grown frail, wasting from some disease. It was only right that Marareta should visit him before he passes, so I sent him." She nodded in approval of her decision. "I pray he returns in time to see another life begin."

Ranadi sobbed almost imperceptibly on hearing these words, and pressed closer against me. Ah, that she was emotional I knew, despite her discipline. I put an arm around her, knowing nothing better to do.

"Mehetu is off to meet her son at the house of the High King. She may bring Pua back too. Again, they had best hurry back!" She laughed at her jest and then gave me a long look. Thinking of how Mehetu and I had parted, no doubt.

"Is anyone here, Lady Panoha?" I asked, smiling.

"Tita is about. She definitely does not want to miss the birth of her little sister."

"Sister?" Ranadi looked wonderingly up at me. "How does she know?"

"There was a prophecy. I'll tell you that tale some day."

"Know that you have chosen to associate with some quite strange people, young lady," spoke Panoha. "Wizards and wanderers and tellers of tales." She gazed for a moment out over her gardens. "We shall eat in a bit. Why don't you two go get cleaned up or whatever and join me later?"

We went to do just that, first locating an unoccupied sleeping chamber. "I like Panoha," said Ranadi. "Could she adopt me?"

"Adoption is not a thing done casually nor for convenience. It would not do to ask her for it; she must offer to take you into her family."

Ranadi busied herself with finding a clean kilt in her pack before saying, "I think that is sensible. Otherwise it would be meaningless. It would be something bought and sold in the marketplace!"

"You understand."

She giggled. "Maybe I am starting to think like a Mora."

"You do know you will have to have tattoos if you become part of a family," I warned. "Especially a noble one."

The girl cocked her head at me. "Could not I simply get the tattoos? Then everyone would think I belonged to a noble family!"

I thought that quite scandalous. It was also quite true. "If you were found out — hmm, in the old days you would have been put to death. Painfully, I think. I do not know what would happen now. It is just not done!"

"It would be as bad as asking to be adopted, wouldn't it?" She did not need to think long on that. "Very well. If I am to be Mora I shall follow the rules."

She just might do that. But being who she was, Ranadi also might not.

199

54. Epics

"I am a woman now and may eat with the adults," Tita informed me. The girl had reached perhaps thirteen years of age but already stood taller than Ranadi. In time, she would tower over her. Of that I had no doubt.

The five of us dined there on the porch where we had been greeted by Panoha. The lady apparently did not move much from one spot. I had to direct Ranadi to the proper seating place. There was so much she had to learn of our customs!

There were tales to be told, spoken in the pidgin so Ranadi might not be left out. Courtesy and hospitality are important to my people. I related my story of Taki and how he had ended up. "Not quite material for an epic, my friend," was Ulani's assessment.

"But I'm glad he's happy now," chimed in Tita. "Even if he is a great oaf."

When we had our fill of roast duck and yams, millet beer and many kinds of fruit, Ulani announced that he would sing one of the old traditional epics on the front porch. "Come, my radiant Ranadi," he invited, "and learn of our legends."

"Go," I told her. "I will speak with the Lady Panoha for a while longer." That this had been planned by the two, I had not the least doubt.

Tita sat quietly, cross-legged, a short distance away from us.

"Ranadi is not your wife, is she?" asked Panoha.

"No, nor have we spoken of marriage. I would marry her if she wanted it of me."

"You see an obligation to provide for her." The wife of Marareta understood that exceedingly well. "But you do not love her."

"Perhaps not as I should." I did care for her. Maybe I could be happy with her. But could she be happy with me?

"And what of Mehetu?"

"She was often in my thoughts as I traveled," I admitted. "But I can not claim to love her either. She is — a fond memory."

"Mehetu thinks of you, as well. We have spoken together at times of what might be. Do you still seek, Hito?"

"I do. But I have learned that what I seek can not be found far away. It may be by the shores of A'auwa."

"At the shrine of Teva. Do not be surprised I know this, my friend. My husband visits with the priest Hoka from time to time."

Of course. Marareta would understand. Did he not himself so seek, once? "I could offer little as a husband if I chose that life." I had never admitted aloud that I might.

"You could offer yourself. That may be enough." She called to her daughter. "Tita, find a servant, will you? I think I will go to my bed chamber now." To me she said, "Go listen to Ulani and hold that little girl. Your doubts can wait until tomorrow."

I found Ranadi where a few members of the household sat listening on the front steps. She would understand almost none of Ulani's story, as it was not only in Mora but an old-fashioned Mora. "I must learn your tongue," she whispered as I took a place beside her. "Perhaps Ulani could teach me."

"I do not think we will stay long enough for that." A possible solution presented itself to me. "Unless you would wish to remain when I travel on."

Did she sigh, ever so slightly? "Where do you go now, Hito?"

"Down the river to the sea. Some of your people are likely to be there." How she would feel about that, I had no idea. "I shall return to this house soon."

"I think I would rather go with you," she decided.

Tita plopped down beside us. "I think Toare would like you," she told Ranadi. "If you wish to rid yourself of this fellow."

Ranadi nodded. "I hear he is very handsome." She could not long keep a straight face, nor could Tita, and both snickered.

"He is too young for you," I informed her.

"Not that much younger," objected Tita. It was true; I was as much older than the Kohari dancer as Toare was younger. And that was somewhat less than the difference between me and his mother!

"Well, Hito, you said we would return here. Perhaps I can learn the Mora language from this handsome boy then."

"You leave again?" asked the Mora girl. "You only arrived!"

"Not for long. I go to visit your uncle at the Great Falls."

"He sent some of your belongings here," said Tita. "No one thought to tell you."

"Oh, my sword. I shall leave that here for now, along with my load of trade goods. Do feel free to choose a pot or two for yourself and your mother, my lady."

"I thank you, Warrior Hito." She grinned at me. "I have already looked them all over, of course."

55. Calm Days

Ranadi should know more of my land and my people before making any decisions about her life. We took canoe the next morning, to further her education. Teoma grew ever wider as we floated down toward Lake Aedina and there was much on either side to catch the girl's attention and interest, the houses of prosperous farmers, fields and orchards, folk of all ages swimming in the river. These would wave in a friendly manner as we passed and some young men also called out for us to stop a while!

It was nearly noon when she asked, "Your friends in that house were all nobles of your people, were they not?"

"It is so."

"But you are not."

"That also is true, Ranadi."

"The servants told me you would not have been allowed to eat with nobles in some houses. That is not the way of the Kohari."

"I did not know that. About your people, that is." I was nearly as ignorant of the Kohari as she of the Mora. "They are not traditionalists in the house of Marareta. Nor," I continued, "where we are going."

She was silent for some time. I paddled on, not at all strenuously for the river's flow was strong. "I was also told that you — ah, courted one who lived there."

That Ranadi was bound to learn. "I did not. But once I thought I might on my return to this land."

"And now?"

"Now there is you." She could make what she wished of that. I was not myself sure what I meant by it. There was little more conversation on that trip.

"That is the house of King Va'aru." I pointed across the long narrow lake we had entered, Aedina which lay above the Great Falls. "We do not stop there now. Maybe on our way back."

"It is bigger than the house of Marareta," she observed. "Or of Gordie."

"Taller yet stands the house of the High King," I told her. "That, too, you shall see some day." I steered us down the lake and toward the right side, across from the king's house. Many canoes of many lengths rested there.

"We walk from here," I told her, pulling our craft up onto the shore. "It is not too far."

"Do we need to carry food?" asked Ranadi. Perhaps she thought we began another expedition.

"We should feast with Lord Temani'itu tonight," I replied. It was yet early in the day; we should easily reach the house of all who sail the sea before nightfall. "But a snack would not be a bad idea."

Past the upper falls, those that fell from the northern end of Aedina, we passed. Those could not be seen so well from our path. "They roar like a great animal," said Ranadi. "I can hear nothing else!"

I would not tell her of the Great Falls, where Teoma took its final dive into the sea. She would behold them soon enough. So, in time, we reached the cliffs, and those who both guarded the ropes and hoisted anything that required it. Ranadi watched a man clambering up for a moment.

"A basket?" asked one, eyeing the girl. I thought that a good idea.

Ranadi did not. "When I am old and fat I shall need to be lowered like a bag of yams," she stated, and let herself down one of the dangling lines. I saw much admiration in the attendants' eyes before following her to the beach below.

She stood on the sand, staring toward the falls. "They are very beautiful, Hito," she whispered. "Could we live here?"

"Only if you become one of Temani'itu's sailors. Then you would have to go far out onto the sea whenever he ordered it." I managed not to break into a grin as I said this.

"You are cruel to tease me so! Maybe one of these large men will thrash you for me." A number of Mora seamen stood about, many looking at us. Ah, mostly looking at Ranadi, it is true.

"Is the Lord Temani'itu in your house?" I asked of them. He could be out sailing.

"He is. He will be pleased to see you again, Hito." It was to be expected that some would remember me; more than once had I visited here.

It seemed a fine day, calm, warm. The sun was falling into the sea before us, falling from a sky with a few high thin clouds. The sea itself was not so calm, for high waves broke on the sand bars. To the long, low, open house I brought Ranadi and there presented her to Temani'itu, where he sat upon a mat, smoking and gazing out to sea.

His greeting was cordial enough, but the old sailor seemed preoccupied, his eyes turning again and again toward the west. "I have seen days like this," he said. "Calm days. Sometimes a storm follows them."

56. Warnings

"Your Lord Temani'itu is the biggest Mora I had seen yet," said Ranadi, perching sideways on her hammock. She seemed to have slept well in it — I only fell out of mine twice!

"You might go long without seeing one larger." I could think of no more than a handful of men.

"I would have to stand on my own shoulders to look him in the face," she declared. "What do we do today?"

"We might visit the traders who come from your homeland. This place is also a trade village of sorts."

Ranadi screwed up her face but made no comment. Being around traders again probably didn't sound like much fun. "I'm hungry," she said. "When I am full, you may take me where you please."

I wanted Ranadi to know she could always visit here if she yearned to hear Kohari voices. Her homeland was forever gone, a place she could not set foot.

The surf thundered even louder on the beach. There was a bank of cloud out over the sea, touched red here and there by the sun that rose over the cliffs. The two of us shared pieces of papaya from a bowl I carried, and walked along the sand.

"Are there crocodiles in here?" asked Ranadi when we reached the edge of the lagoon.

"No, only sharks."

"They eat people too, do they not?" It hadn't occurred to me that she would know nothing of them. The shark was no more than a creature of mythology to her.

"It happens, but they will not come out of the water after you. Come, we can cross under the falls."

I feared the damp passageway below the Great Falls, full of mist and spray, would dampen Ranadi as well, but she laughed and held her arms out into the spray. That made me nervous for Ranadi was not a swimmer. Something else she should be taught, that was.

But it was good that she might delight in such things. At moments such as those I could believe I loved her.

As we approached the camp of the traders there was a hush, and wide-eyed stares. "It is the girl he stole from the temple!" I could hear someone say.

"Welcome, Hero!" came a greeting.

"Hail, Poyo." The man grinned at me but the looks of those behind him were almost reverential. I had a reputation now, among these people — a people with no love for the priests or the temple.

"And this is the dancer?" he asked. "Definitely worth kidnapping."

"No, sir," Ranadi told him. "It was I who kidnapped Hito." The man laughed deeply, his curling gray beard wagging up and down.

"Come," he said. "Is it too early for palm wine?" Poyo contemplated that question only a moment before answering for himself. "No, of course not. It is never too early!"

To Ranadi, he said, "Look over my wares. Perhaps you will see something Hito would like to buy for you." He chuckled over that. Then his eyes went to the girl's necklace. "Ah, I recognize those stones, Hito."

"Those are what got me into trouble, my friend, trying to discover their source. I can blame you for all of it!"

"Or thank me for sending you to find this jewel instead." He handed me a bowl of wine. It would be customary, I knew, for one of the women to offer refreshment to Ranadi. The Kohari, too, had their ways.

"You had best not let Rika see her," warned Poyo. My old friend had accompanied Marareta on his journey south and had not been at his house. Yes, he would enjoy gazing upon Ranadi, at least when his wife was not present.

Ha, he would not nag me about finding a woman again!

Someone had handed Ranadi a small bowl. She looked at the oblong box at Poyo's side, and told him, "I have not heard the sef in a long time. It was not one of the instruments played at the temple."

"Then shall I play for you," he said, picking it up. For a moment he played with the pegs that protruded at the one end, plucking at the three strings. Then Poyo launched into one of the Kohari's incomprehensible songs.

"Dance for us," someone called.

Ranadi began to move in the intricate steps of her sacred dance; then abruptly she stopped and stared around her, chest heaving. "I shall never dance again," she sobbed and ran from us. My Kohari friends surely understood why I followed without making a farewell.

No word did I say when I reached her, bent, weeping, by the lagoon, but only took her in my arms. "I suddenly realized how greatly my life has changed," she whispered. "Let us go back to your Mora friends. They are my people now."

She stood straight and without tears by the time we returned to the house of those who sail the sea. The banked clouds had climbed higher, blocking out half the sky now. The wind seemed fitful, blowing along the cliff face, sometimes almost calm, sometimes gusting.

"Lord Naio!" someone called. Men pointed toward the open water. There, a sail rose and fell among the swells.

"Temani'itu was concerned," said an old man standing near us, one of the fishermen who sailed from this beach. "He fears there is storm coming." He looked to the sky. "As do I."

Could Naio's canoe make it through the breaking waves? I am no sailor; this I have said before. But it was a good Mora canoe, one of medium size, and the men aboard it were skilled. Toward the lagoon they were angling, where the waters of the Teoma met the sea. Ah, the waves lost much of their power on the outer sandbars there, did they not? A swell rose beneath the hull, the men paddled mightily, and then they were carried along by it, sliding into the deeper water of the inlet. A crowd gathered about them as they brought their canoe onto the sand.

Perhaps that was something done every day here. I would not wish to take such a chance! "Let us go to Lord Temani'itu," I said to Ranadi. "Naio will surely report to him."

57. The Storm

"It is coming," warned Naio. "We fled before the storm."

"As must we, now," Temani'itu spoke. "Get everyone atop the cliffs and try to secure the canoes."

"What of the Kohari?" someone asked. "It is forbidden for them to pass the cliffs." This had been so ever since the war three years before.

There was no question for the Mora leader. "We must let them come up. Poneiva may complain later if he wishes."

"I will tell them, Lord Temani'itu," I said. "I think they might more readily believe me." He nodded an agreement. "Remain here," I told Ranadi. "Assist if you can but do not get in the way."

I didn't even wait for an acknowledgment from her before running toward the traders' camp. Other Mora ran with me; there were fishermen over there to be warned, too.

Soon I was explaining all to the Kohari who gathered around me.

"Our boats —" objected one.

A Mora sailor who had accompanied me said, "You must do as we. Fill them with stones and hope they survive."

"Gather what you can carry and cross under the falls," I ordered. "Women right now, and the children." Best to get them out of the way. They stood there, uncertain.

"You have heard him!" shouted Poyo. "Get to it."

Soon, I was leading one group, and then another along the way behind the falling Teoma. Most of the Kohari had never walked there, as they rarely passed to that side of the beach. Temani'itu had taken up a position by the cliffs, supervising the evacuation up the ropes. It was a bit surprising to see Ranadi at his side, and occasionally scurrying off on some errand for him. Delivering messages, maybe, or checking progress.

I watched another Kohari woman go up in a basket and then turned to the sea. Black was the sky and the waves rolled ever higher on the sands. Had we waited a little longer, many might have died here. Many still might, I realized, including me.

Naio was speaking to Temani'itu. "You should go, my lord," said his second. "I can finish things."

Temani'itu would not hear of it. "I am responsible for all who are here. It is for me to see to their safety." He turned to Ranadi, just returned. "You should go now, child," he rumbled.

"I will stay with you," she insisted. "I can climb quickly when it is needed."

I turned to go gather more Kohari and anyone else still on the beach. There was rain now, off and on, driving rain. This was no doing of Teva! Which god I should blame, I was uncertain — there was a god of thunder and one of the sea and one of storms. I think all three were working together that day. Maybe the Great Shark Wanga was helping too.

There were cries. There, a great wall, a wave, hurtling toward the beach. It would sweep far up the sand, perhaps all the way to the cliffs themselves. "To the falls!" I yelled as loudly as I might. "Leave everything else!" Alas, there were those who would not listen and walk no more with men.

Those who made it there, or near to the cliffs, were safe. But the next surge would surely be higher; all should leave now. I gazed southward along the sand, in a world growing dark as night, and saw none. "Let us go," I told this last band of refugees and we crossed under the falls and hurried toward the hanging ropes.

Lord Temani'itu was being hoisted up in a commodious basket even as we approached, Ranadi climbing beside him. Looking about, I saw only able men. We could all climb, the last to leave.

Where to? I had no idea. But it was certainly safer atop the cliffs than below them. I climbed when my turn came, and the last of the Mora followed. Naio stood there, making sure all made it safely. "Most are already marching toward the house of Va'aru," he said, "Temani'itu in his litter." I would not wish to be bearing the massive man anytime, much less in this weather.

"Is my woman about?" I asked. "Ranadi?"

"She walks beside the lord. He asked this of her." That was acceptable to me. So we, too, began the trek to Aedina and the house of King Va'aru. Perhaps we could make it before the wind and rain became too great and we were forced to take shelter along the way. I knew of these great storms, had seen them come ravening up the valley of the Teoma, but had never been at the coast when one struck.

How we might pass over Aedina when we reached it was also a mystery to me. Surely the waters would be too rough by then. There was a narrow suspension bridge further up this valley, hanging high above the Teoma, but only a fool would attempt that in these winds. And most certainly a litter bearing Lord Temani'itu could not cross.

"There is usually more warning," said Naio, who walked beside me in this rear guard. "This storm came straight in from the sea instead of along the coast."

"Then we were fortunate to get everyone away. Almost everyone." I said a silent prayer for the few who did not make it.

"Yes. Seeing it heading in convinced most they needed to run!" He gazed at the skies for a long time before speaking again. "It will get far worse but I think we will make it to Va'aru in time. If not, there are shelters along the way for just such times."

I saw those shelters as we passed them, sturdy huts partially sunken into a hillside. A few men turned aside and entered them. "They will stay and keep an eye on the path," my noble companion told me. "Someone might become lost or need aid." There had been many storms over many years, and the Mora who sailed from the Great Falls had learned the lessons they taught.

How late was it when we reached Aedina? I know not for the sun was hidden, but I would guess it was near dusk. Many canoes and rafts were already ferrying people across, guided by thick ropes stretching all the way across the lake. The rain and the darkness was thick by the time I crossed over, one of the last, and the water of Aedina was starting to stand on end.

58. Announcements

"I shall go to the house of Marareta," announced Temani'itu. "I leave you in charge here, Naio."

The Mora noble showed no surprise, simply nodding in agreement. Outside, the storm yet howled and battered at King Va'aru's home.

"I think it is letting up," opined that king. "The eye missed us."

"It went to visit Hei'iro, maybe," said Lord Temani'itu. I sat well behind that man, with Ranadi leaning against me. There were many people packed into Va'aru's great hall, not all of them Mora.

"And then on to the Salt Coast," said Naio. "No man can guess where a storm might turn."

Temani'itu turned, trying to pick me out in the darkness. "Hito, you will travel with me, will you not? And Ranadi."

"Certainly, my lord," I called back.

"Good." He turned back to his companions, king and high noble. "One canoe only shall I take and two or three men. And —" He leaned in and whispered something I could not make out. This time the face of Naio did show surprise.

But he nodded and turned back to his bowl of beer. I could have used some of that, myself. "You were brave today," I told Ranadi.

"I am always brave," she objected. "Oh, almost always." Maybe she remembered the griffins.

"Such a storm brought my people here, in the old legends," I told her. "The Taona Marareta says that he and his comrades arrived in the same way."

"Do you think he will be at his house when we return? I would like to meet him."

"It is possible."

By the middle of the next day, we could all get outside and begin cleaning up and repairing or just giving thanks that it was over. There was little rain though the wind was still strong at times.

Ranadi and I were among those who had no other obligation than to give thanks. "Most of Va'aru's roof is still intact," I noted. "Not so some of the other buildings." It is not difficult to replace some thatch, though inconvenient if one is taking shelter in a building when it blows away.

A Mora hurried over to let us know, "Temani'itu is leaving tomorrow morning."

"We'll be ready," I replied. He hurried off to tell someone else something else. "I think the traders will be heading back to the beach tomorrow too," I said. "It is to be hoped their boats were not destroyed."

"And if they are?"

"They will have to move in with us. We shall build an extremely large house for all of them."

She shook her head at me. "I think maybe you would, if you could. I am sorry I ran away from them."

"You need not run anymore, Ranadi."

"I hope that is so." As did I.

Temani'itu was, as promised, ready to go at dawn, he and three warriors in a large canoe, Ranadi and I in our smaller one. We remained abreast much of the way and even conversed some, canoe to canoe. There was some damage along the way, and much debris afloat. Here and there a fallen tree might be spied, or a roofless hut.

The Teoma was swollen but ran not so high as at the height of rainy season, nor was its flow so swift. We reached the village by the house of Marareta in good time, a busy village as its people worked at cleanup and repair. "The taona is at his house," one called as we disembarked. "He arrived with the storm!"

Temani'itu was not so old a man — of little more than five tens were his years — but he was very fat and did not move with ease. We must keep to his pace as he progressed up the path to the house, a pace slowed further when he would stop and look about at the groves and grounds from time to time. There seemed almost a longing in his gaze. "The house of Marareta is always a pleasant place to visit," he said. "So was it too when it was the house of Hareata." The man had spent much time there; Temani'itu and Hareata had been both great friends and political allies.

That someone had run ahead of us to announce our coming was obvious, for Marareta waited before his porch. "Greetings, Taona," spoke the old sailor. "Your wife is well?"

"She is, and certain to give me a child any time now. Excuse her for not coming to greet you, Temmi."

"Panoha has a more important arrival to concern herself with!" A deep, rumbling chuckle came from the big man. "Is my sister here?" A pair of his warriors stood close as he climbed the steps, ready to lend aid if needed.

"No, nor the Lady Mehetu." Marareta turned to Ranadi and me.

"I welcome you to my house. Your companion is as beautiful as I was told, Friend Hito."

"Brave, too," asserted Temani'itu. He sat himself down on one of the mats there on the porch. "Let us talk here. You, too," he said, motioning Ranadi and me to him.

"Taona," I asked, "what news is there of Samua?"

"Samua has left this world." Servants appeared, with bowls of beer and of fruit. "He was never completely well," continued Marareta, directing the attendants where to place the refreshments. "A hard life had Samua, and he drank more than he should. It was good that he found peace in his last years, here in this land."

Temani'itu nodded gravely at this. "Good, indeed." He took a great gulp of beer before speaking further. "This storm showed me I can no longer serve as I have. It is time to leave the sea, to spend my days in a house like yours, Marareta, watching my gardens grow.

"I go to Poneiva to tell him this and ask him to name Naio in my place. Then I shall go to my own house that is now so often empty. There is one," he continued, "I would ask to go with me."

He turned his broad, heavy-browed face to Ranadi. "I would make you one of my family if you are willing, Ranadi," he stated. "Would you be my daughter?"

59. Comings and Goings

"This is what we wanted for you," I said. A small oil lamp lit our chamber.

"But I must leave you and go live in the house of Temani'itu." Her smile came mingled with sadness. "I must learn to be Mora."

"Not only Mora but a Mora noblewoman."

"Has Temani'itu no family?"

"His children are grown and his wives come and go. It would not be expected they would always reside in his house when he was so often absent himself." I thought then to add, "There is his sister, the Lady Pua."

"I think I am frightened of meeting her. She seems very important."

"She was." Not so much now.

"Once you wished to be important. Oh, I know this, Hito. Now you seek something else." I had no ready answer to this. "You want to go and live in peace and be a priest. I have heard this in your words, even when you did not mean to say it."

"This may be so. Perhaps that life, too, will not satisfy me."

"But you must try it. That is a journey you must undertake without me, Hito."

"I know this." I had not admitted it but, yes, I had known it.

"So I have learned from you and now shall learn from another. This is not a bad thing, is it?" There was just the slightest tone of pleading in her voice. My approval was needed still.

"It is not. We have each learned much from the other, little Tamba." Never again, I was sure, would I call her that. We would not travel as companions again.

"Let us say goodbye," she whispered, blowing out the light. "At least for a while."

I found the Lady Pua at dawn, taking an early breakfast on the side porch. "My brother has told me many things," was her greeting. "We arrived in the night and Temmi wished to talk. Now I wish to talk with you. Sit."

Wordlessly, I took a place to her right. "I shall go with your Ranadi and my brother when they depart, and dwell a while in his house." Pua paused before asking, "Is she still your Ranadi?"

"My lady, I am not sure she ever was."

"Ah. I think Mehetu will be pleased to hear that."

"She is not mine either." There was no reason for me to say that. "Mehetu accompanied you, my lady?"

"Yes. She is with Panoha, I think." A faint smile touched her lips. "They are much better friends to each other than they will ever be to me." She busied herself with a slice of melon before continuing. "Tell me of Ranadi."

How to start? "She is frivolous and vain and self-centered, and also serious and practical and courageous. She is highly disciplined — Ranadi will learn the role of Temani'itu's daughter well." Then I had to laugh. "But she will never look like a member of your family, Lady Pua. She is a tiny woman."

"This I had heard. Also that men find her good to look upon."

"I must admit that I do." From the start. "She is perhaps not truly beautiful but there is a — vitality to Ranadi."

Pua nodded. I believe she understood what I said. "My son must be around somewhere," she said. "I would spend time with him before I hurry away again."

"He is to be Toare's master, I have heard."

"That is so. They will want to hear all your adventures while you are here and craft some preposterous epic of them."

A servant came and whispered in the lady's ear. Pua nodded. "I shall be there shortly," she told her and the woman hurried away. "It seems Tita's sibling is about to arrive," she announced. "I should be there." She did not sound overly enthusiastic about it.

I idly wondered if Ranadi had ever been present at a birth. Pua left a few moments later and then, one by one, the men of the household began to show up, looking for breakfast. Marareta appeared nervous, and came and went. Ha, the man had been on the other side of the mountains when his first child was born, a child he did not know Pana'a was carrying. He would not escape so easily this time!

Ulani and Toare sat with me and indeed wished to hear my tales. As I spun one out for them, that of my time in the Kohari temple, I spied Temani'itu joining us. Ranadi was at his side. Toare's attention frequently strayed from me after that.

I wondered then if Ranadi had intentionally charmed the old sailor, hoping for just such an adoption or, at least, to be in the good graces of a high noble. Was that a stretch? It was not beyond her, certainly.

Through the morning, the girl left and returned several times.

Serving as her adopted father's messenger again, I suspected, bringing news of Panoha. At last, she whispered in his ear and the big man smiled widely. But it would be for Marareta to make an announcement.

That was no more than, "Rahiri has arrived. Her mother is well." He abruptly disappeared again. Not long after, Pua came and sat with us.

"That is done." She turned to Ulani. "How goes it with you, beloved?"

"Well, my mother. I like it here." He grinned at Toare. "I have yet to learn if my new apprentice has any skill."

"That has never prevented many storytellers from opening their mouths," I observed.

Pua laughed. "There is the Hito of old." She looked about. "Ranadi has flitted away again? She seemed very excited about all this."

"She grew up in a temple and knows little of the world," I told them. "Many things are new to her, and exciting. Ranadi is amazingly ignorant for so bright a girl."

The noblewoman nodded. "My brother is rising. I think he means to leave soon. We have had no time together, Ulani."

"Perhaps I shall come visit the house of Temani'itu," he replied. "My apprentice would approve."

Within the hour, goodbyes had been made to Marareta and all who dwelt in this house, and Temani'itu was on his way to the river. Only Toare, Ulani, and I accompanied his party that far; there was much to keep everyone else busy.

And so I embraced Ranadi farewell, and Ulani embraced Lady Pua, and Toare stood looking a bit embarrassed. "I wish she could have remained longer," said the boy, as the canoes disappeared up the Teoma.

I could not help but agree. I turned and whispered, "Goodbye," one last time.

60. Peace

All these events were factors in my decision, the storm, the loss of Ranadi, even the death of Samua. They pushed me further toward choosing to become a priest.

For a few days longer would I linger in the house of Marareta. More of that time I spent with Rika and Hepetea, and their baby, than with my noble friends.

Could I even call them friends? Marareta, yes. The women I would not have even known were it not for the taona. There would be nothing between Mehetu and me. The noblewoman would not know my name, nor would she wish to.

Little I saw of her for some time, for she remained with Panoha and the new child, the little girl. Yet on the evening of the second day, she came to where I sat on the porch, looking out on the gardens. Fragrant were those gardens.

"My son tells me you have reached the conclusion of a great story," Mehetu spoke, taking a place by my side.

"Who can be sure of that? Lives do not wrap themselves up as neatly as the epics of the storytellers."

"But you rest now, do you not, Hito? Or are you still searching?"

"Do I search? Maybe. I have searched far this past year and much have I found. Yes, and lost as well."

"She is truly gone then?" Mehetu knew what I had lost.

"Gone, as I always knew she would be someday. Yet I regret it not, neither the journeys nor the loss, for they have pointed out a way for me."

"A way that leads to the shores of A'auwa."

"For now. I seek the chance of peace." The chance — yes, just that was enough. "My eyes were opened among the Kohari. What I have seen of their fighting and vendettas makes me see my own people anew. Our ancestors may not have been so different from them."

Mehetu nodded in agreement. She knew much of the Mora past, had sought out the tales that few now sang. "There was much evil in the old days. Maybe it lives yet in our hearts, for we still war."

"I turned from war, saying it was to seek my fortune as a trader, but it was peace I truly sought. Now I turn to the service of a god to seek further."

"I think that is good thing, Hito," Mehetu said. She rose and reentered the house.

Of Mehetu's son, I saw a great deal more, for he and Ulani must have all my story. I avoided embellishment; they would surely add their own. But telling it all, thinking again of those days, brought ever more to me the need to continue my search — continue it where it had started, at A'auwa.

And so I took my leave of Marareta and of his house, of Rika and Hepetea, of Panoha and Tita. I said my farewells to Ulani and Toare. To Mehetu, I said farewell last of all, standing on the banks of Teoma, and even held her in my arms, though we had not again become lovers.

"It is the time that I must return to A'auwa, and to the shrine of Teva to see if that is my place. Whether I stay a season or a lifetime,

225

I do not know."

"I could share such a life, Hito. I might even long, as do you, to leave the cares of this house, of my life, and seek peace." There would be more to say, I knew, and I waited. "My life is here for now, with my son. But in time, who could know?"

"Then for that too shall I wait a season or a lifetime," I told her.

I pushed my canoe out onto Teoma's rain-misted flow. Teva's shrine lay ahead, and the house of old Hoka.

An Afterword

This novel is a sequel, of sorts, to my 'Malvern' trilogy, the tales of castaway Michael Malvern, who came to be known as Marareta. Hito's story has come to a close but there will be more novels set among the Mora.

Kuru, for any who might have wondered, is breadfruit. It was carried widely by Polynesians, which, of course, the Mora are. Whereas the ancestors of the Kohari and the Diwarna would have arrived completely by accident, a few individuals at a time swept into a new world, the Mora were purposely migrating, exiles seeking a home, and would have brought animals and crop plants with them.

Stephen Brooke

Author and artist Stephen Brooke lives and works in an old farmhouse in the Florida Panhandle. All his books are available from Arachis Press, a small publisher dedicated to presenting meaningful literature for readers of all ages.

Visit http://arachispress.com for our catalog.